MILITIA
MEN

MILITIA MEN

Published by Lonely Whale Press
Astoria, Oregon

©2023 by William Dean
All rights reserved

Cover and Interior Design by We Got You Covered Book Design

ISBN: 978-1-7373452-9-9

MILITIA MEN

A NOVEL

WILLIAM DEAN

FOR ANN

"I'M NO HERO. I'M A SURVIVOR."

ALEXANDRA AUSTIN
UNITED STATES SENATOR

PROLOGUE

DO YOU HAVE *any regrets?*

What a dumb question.

Regrets? Oh yeah, I'm drowning in them.

There's no escape. This place is a deep, murky pool of regret and all you can do is tread water, wishing things had gone down differently, or yield to the pain and drown. Two choices. Two levels of hell.

"So many," I answer in a tiny voice. "Too many."

You seem tense.

She's looking at my hands and I realize that I'm gripping the edges of the square sofa cushion so hard my knuckles are white and my fingernails are buried deep in the fabric, a faded cream. It's an ugly couch, not well-suited for a shrink's office because it's not even long enough to lie on. But nothing is what it should be here. Everything is a terrible version of itself. Especially me.

"Sorry," I say, willing my fingers to unlatch. They slowly do.

What would you have done differently?

"Everything." The word comes out sounding vaguely hopeful, like the start of a confession. "I'd have done just about everything

1

differently."

I brave a faint smile. She writes something in her notes and it makes me gulp because I have to get out and she holds the key. I miss freedom and its quirks. I even miss the homeless people who pushed their shopping carts every day in front of my shop. I don't think I'd shoo them away anymore if I was free. I'd get to know them … if I was truly alive again.

My heart beats a little faster. The first beads of sweat are forming. All this treading water. I start squeezing the cushion again.

"I wouldn't have gone to Portland that night. I wouldn't have let him join."

More scribbles in the pad on her lap. She says nothing, just lets the silence float there like an ambiguous cloud, one with the power to either bring rain or allow sunshine.

"I … I don't want to talk about Sean anymore."

It's a plea, not a request. A numbered man in an orange jumpsuit doesn't have much sway. Actually, he's got none at all.

Her face remains a blank. A freshly painted wall with nothing hanging on it. She taps her pen, peers over the top of her reading glasses.

Why did you make the call, Robb?

I hesitate. Is this a trick question? She's cocked her head, taking stock. Assessing. The air seems thick as pie.

"I was out of options," I say finally. "Nothing I'd tried worked and now she's in the trunk. He's in the passenger seat with the gun. … I had to do *something.*"

Uninvited tears are welling. My head hangs low. The words tear through me like 60-grit sandpaper.

"It wasn't an act of courage. I was desperate, that's all."

Desperate for what?

"To stop him. To save her." I look up, begging her to stop with my eyes. "To save myself."

CHAPTER
ONE
ROBB

WE WERE STONERS in high school, me and Sean.

There was a covered place behind the old gym where we could fire one up and not be seen. A blind spot. We called it "The Office" because we put in regular hours. We thought that was hilarious.

Sometimes the janitor, Ancient Al, would join us for a couple of tokes and reminisce about his glory days in a blues band on one gritty side of Chicago or another. South or east, I could never keep it straight. We enjoyed his stories, though. For a wrinkled old dude with a kinky Santa beard, he was cool. We liked getting high and listening to him play the trumpet.

Jocks would stop by after practice to buy a few Js, which put some cash in our pockets. We sold them shitty, throat-scouring weed for about five times what it cost us. Dumb asses. The hot chicks? We'd give them our best pot for free if they were chill. So, definitely not the stuck-up cheerleaders or student government clones or anyone with a GPA over 3.5.

Except Layla Meadows.

She moved to our tidy Oregon town in senior year. Her Hippie parents named her after the Clapton song, she told us with one of her trademark shrugs that seemed to say "whatever." She grew up in an orange VW camper van, roaming the country, back and forth, and then back again. Never staying in one place for long. Her mom and dad were basically minstrels, playing guitar and performing one-act plays they'd written themselves. Donations dropped into a striped Seuss hat paid for food and gas.

At Astoria High, she was a rule-busting rebel, which I guess is why she'd skip class now and then to hang with us. She was always super friendly, which is saying something because she was hard-core Goth back then, with body ink and piercings and the whole nine yards, down to her racoon eyes and the red streak running through her black hair.

Layla was also really smart – an honor student. That amazed Sean and me since we never once saw her with a textbook or heard her ask a single question in class. She'd just sit in the back row, drawing stuff in the sketch pad she always carried around. Mostly swirly, mystical things that flowed from her imagination. Van Gogh on acid. I'd sneak a peek once in a while and she'd catch me, then flip me off under her desk. That always cracked me up.

The three of us became good friends. Sean liked how she played shooter games and bowled like a guy. I just liked her. Kissed her once when we were drunk. Made her laugh, which didn't exactly do wonders for my confidence. But back then I was too shy or stupid to do anything about it.

Next thing I knew, she was off to some art school in Seattle.

I figured I'd never see her again, but four years later she finds me at the River Vista somehow. Knocks on the door to No. 1 – my door. Complete surprise.

Same raven hair, but now with rivulets of deep blue. Same warm brown eyes, mahogany inlaid with flakes of gold. Same sly smile, only sexier.

"Robb, ya doof," she said. "How ya been?"

A month later, she moves into the vacant apartment on the top floor. Turns it into an art studio. Starts creating swirly, mystical things. On canvas this time.

I had just opened Spoke & Wheel a few blocks away in a neglected part of downtown where down-and-outers camped on the sidewalk under awnings. But I was proud of it. I invited her to come over and check it out: the handful of new and used bikes for sale in front; modest repair shop in back.

She toured the fledgling business that had drained all my savings with something approaching awe.

"Holy crap! You're an entrepreneur!"

God, how I wanted to kiss her just then. That wouldn't happen until a full year later when I finally worked up the courage to ask her out. Fish and chips from a boat converted into a food truck, followed by free live music at one of the nearby breweries. Cheap date, but she loved it.

When we returned to the River Vista, she grabbed me. Pushed me against the wall in the lobby. We kissed like fire.

After that and a few more cheap dates, she became my girl.

The trouble with Sean started a couple of years later. Truth be told, it was Layla who introduced him to True Patriots, though nobody could have foreseen what would happen. Certainly not me.

One day, I hear this banging on my door, and it's her, out of breath from sprinting down two flights of stairs.

She grabs me by both shoulders.

"Road trip. Portland. Right now. Get dressed."

I thought I *was* dressed, so I look down and see that I'm still in my green plaid robe and fuzzy purple slippers. Me and Sean were playing the new Call of Duty and kinda lost track of time, which is not at all unusual for us.

"Hey, girl," Sean mutters from the couch. He waves a greasy, half-spent bag of Taco Bell chips. "Nacho?"

"Boys, we gotta go," she says urgently, handing me her phone. The screen is filled with a news story, which I find surprising since Layla lives in her own world and doesn't often bother herself with dispatches from the outside.

I scroll down, read that an Oregon militia group is planning a "motorcade" in downtown Portland.

Handing the phone back, I make the mistake of yawning. It wasn't the story. I'd been playing COD with Sean for four hours straight, taking turns on the high-def battlefield.

Layla shoots me her meanest look. "Don't you get it? They're crashing a Black Lives Matter event downtown. *On MLK Day!*"

Her woody eyes narrow.

"All hell's gonna break loose. We gotta check it out."

She stares at the two of us and shakes her head with a mix of love and pity. "I'll even drive."

Sean is interested enough to wander over to the doorway. He tugs his downy beard and scratches his balls through his alien-head pajamas. "Cool," he says. "Isn't it like midnight, though?"

"You lazy assholes!" Layla snaps. "It's 6:30!"

"Cool," repeats Sean, shuffling off to his room. He strips without bothering to close the door. His pasty ass moons us.

"Please ma'am, give me a minute to change," I say, trying to be classy.

With a groan she brushes past. Plucks a Fort George Vortex out of the fridge. Pops the can and takes a gulp.

"Have one of my beers," I say, smiling.

"Thanks," she says, waving me away. "Hurry up."

Minutes later, Sean is sleeping sideways in the back seat of her purple Prius while we roll east down Highway 30, bound for the Rose City, Brewtopia, Stumptown or whatever else Portland is calling itself these days. I've had a chance to read the whole article now and I apologize for failing to grasp the significance of what is about to unfold.

A militia group called True Patriots is doing a drive-through in the heart of the city tonight, on Martin Luther King Day, which has civil rights leaders up in arms. There's talk of a counter-protest and rampant speculation about the possibility of violent clashes.

An expert interviewed by The Oregonian calls True Patriots a "White nationalist extremist group" founded by some ex-Marines who'd previously backed an unsuccessful effort to break off eastern Oregon and fold it into more conservative Idaho. Their top issue: Preserving the right to bear arms. Lots and lots of arms.

I'd never heard of them before, but I did know one thing: If there was going to be a street fight between pissed-off, gun-toting Marines and scrawny, starry-eyed libs, I'd bet on the Marines.

I don't say anything, just nod at the driver, who nods back. I couldn't talk to her anyway. Layla always cranks her classic rock when she's driving, usually with the windows down, which drives the old men on the downtown sidewalks crazy.

I look back at Sean, marvel at how he can sleep through anything. It occurs to me that it's probably how he's been able to get up before dawn every day to work for the garbage company, driving a big truck down narrow streets without it becoming a demolition derby.

Layla surprises me by turning down Nirvana in the middle of "Smells Like Teen Spirit," one of her faves. She's excited and alarmed at the same time. The anarchist side of her is being fed an evening snack.

"Thanks for going. I didn't think you would. War games and all." "You're better than me. You should play with us more."

"Nah, Sean hates losing to a girl.

"That's true."

"Besides, I'd rather fuck myself."

"Oh, *that's* the humming noise. Makes the whole building shake, knocking stuff off the walls. I've gotten complaints."

She chuckles in her hoarse, sexy way. "Well, then you should come upstairs more often. You know, do some building maintenance."

My side gig is maintaining the River Vista, where Sean and I share a two-bedroom. The three-story, five-unit building has sat near the corner of Jefferson and 12th for over a century. It's a funky old building, painted lavender and a mossy green, not quite interesting enough to make the historic preservation list, but the views of the Columbia are great – no false advertising there – and tenants are close enough to the waterfront to hear the sea lions bark. Whether they want to or not.

The job calls for minor upkeep, sweeping and mopping the landings and stairs, and putting out the various color-coded trash and recycling carts every week.

For Mrs. Wong, who's 88 and a virtual shut-in, it also means changing her lightbulbs, unclogging her drains and delivering packages and mail from the lobby to her second-floor door. She's nearly blind, so nobody wants her using the stairs much.

For Sean, whose side hustle is selling second-hand furnishings on eBay and Craigslist – stuff he spies on his garbage route and returns later to snag off the sidewalk – it means finding storage space in the building's musty basement. Amazing what people get rid of just because something shinier and newer comes along. Sean calls his efforts "recycling" and I suppose he's right. He's kept a lot of crap out of the landfill. The downside? He's always bugging me to unlock the basement door, since I'm the one with the key.

In the Prius, I look at Layla, study her pretty face for traces of sarcasm. Her tongue gives her upper lip a lick. Good Lord, she's hot even when she's not trying. I rush to say something before she notices that I'm fixated on her mouth.

"Well, if you'd answer your phone or your door more often …"

"I'm probably in the Nest," she says. "Not sorry."

Layla has annexed a part of the roof where she can set up her easel and paint, inspired by the beauty around her. She calls it "The Eagle's Nest." Whenever the weather cooperates, she's there. Sort of off the grid.

"Maybe you can hang a bell and send me down a very long rope," I say, grinning.

"Or you can just shout. Amazing how sounds carry up there."

"The neighbors would love that."

That makes her smile, which always tugs at my heart.

She's my girl, but she can do better. I'm not bad-looking and I went to college, if Clatsop Community and some online business courses count, but Layla … well, she's special. Brainy and talented and gorgeous. The trifecta. She can go places, find some wealthy guy to take her there if she likes. Someone to subsidize her art, get her in a gallery or buy one.

The last thing I want to do is hold her back. Then again, maybe it's true what they say about free spirits like her – that hold on loosely shit. Maybe what's happening with me and Layla is working, and I'm too dumb to know it. Or maybe I'm just insecure.

A while back she gave me one of her paintings to sell on eBay – an abstract portrait of wind and sea that I thought resembled a colorful clash of the gods. She titled it "Evening Ferry Ride." I loved it. I lied and told her it sold for $500 – all I had at the time. I gave her the cash and kept the painting. I honestly can't tell you why. I just had to own a piece of her imagination, I guess.

It's in my closet behind my only sport coat. Whenever I change clothes, I sneak a peek. One of these days I'll hang it over the fireplace in my home.

Our home.

We reach our downtown destination about twenty minutes late after hunting for a place to park, but the motorcade hasn't started yet. The streets by the federal building are filled with angry Black and white people. Mostly white people, since this is Portland after all.

Many of them are carrying professionally printed signs that say **OUT WITH HATE**. I look around for cops and see only a few milling around the federal courthouse. Strange, given the advance warnings.

Layla is noticing the same thing. "Cops have been battling BLM for years at battalion strength, with tear gas, riot shields, rubber bullets … but when the militia rolls through, crickets."

Sean, rubbing sleep from his eyes, joins us. "Maybe they got word that the parade's been canceled."

"You may be right," I say.

"Here they come," Layla says, pointing ahead.

I don't see anything, but I can hear it. The throaty rumble of high-powered vehicles coming our way.

The BLM protesters hear it, too. They'd been listening to a long-haired man with a megaphone exhorting them to rise up against white nationalism, but now they're turning as one to the street. Signs are waving. Fists are clenched.

Then the first vehicle appears – a monstrous 4X4 pickup with full-sized American flags flapping on each side of the stretched bed. On the driver's door is an air-brushed painting of a noble bald eagle and below that the words **TRUE PATRIOTS** in gold.

I squint and make out a sinewy man in an olive drab ballcap and desert-tan fatigues standing proudly in the bed. He's bearded and wearing wraparound sunglasses despite the darkness. He's also cradling a commando-style camo assault rifle, just like Sean's favorite video game avatar. A smile creases the man's face.

Hands reach out to push me to the right. It's Layla jockeying for a better angle for the cellphone video she's shooting.

"You see this guy?" she asks me, not looking up.

"Yeah, he's got a big gun."

"Awesome," Sean says.

Other menacing pickups come into view, with more men in military garb in the beds. They're taunting the protesters now, spitting racist shit. The forest of flags decorating the vehicles make it look like some sort of Bizarro World Fourth of July, even though it's January and cold.

The reaction from the crowd lining the street starts with an angry murmur and quickly builds into something resembling a rolling earthquake. People start shouting and hurling water bottles at the trucks as they pass.

Some of the men in the vehicles take aim with their rifles. It's happening before my eyes, but I can't believe it.

"Oh shit! They're opening fire!"

I look at my friends, thinking we need to take cover. Layla is somehow still filming. Sean seems delighted. Am I the only one who's scared?

People about 50 yards away are getting shot. It's a massacre, another mass shooting going down right in front of us. Adrenalin is pumping.

I'm about to grab Layla by the arm and pull her to safety when I see the people who'd been shot run futilely after the last two trucks. One man turns. There's a bright green splotch on his jacket where a bullet would have pierced his heart.

He'd been paintballed. I look around and see another dozen or so protesters trying to wipe sticky neon paint off their clothes.

As the roar from revved V8s fades, Sean wraps me in a bear hug.

"That was freakin' awesome, man," he says, thrilled by the spectacle. "Those dudes have balls!"

Layla is stunned. "All it would have taken was one guy in the crowd to fire a real gun. And then what would have happened?"

"Some of those militia guys were packing real guns, too," I say. "Assault rifles, pistols … Is that even legal in Oregon?"

"They roll through town and nearly cause a riot," Layla continues, shaking her head. "And nobody gets arrested? Where were the cops?"

The question hangs in the air like wet laundry.

Then Sean sidles up to Layla and smiles.

"Hey, can you send me your video? I gotta see that shit again."

CHAPTER
TWO
ROBB

AFTER PORTLAND, Sean couldn't stop talking about True Patriots.

Putting his PlayStation controller aside – a red flag if ever there was one – he began researching the paramilitary group, eager to learn everything he could.

Layla's video wasn't the only one from that night. Several protesters posted their own, as did the militia itself, off body cams attached to members' uniforms. The captions were wildly different, but all of the clips captured the fury of the demonstrators and the delight of the drive-by disrupters.

But beyond that and the news reports that followed the near-riot there wasn't much in mainstream media for Sean to explore. Tidbits about True Patriots online merely whetted his appetite.

So he dug deeper. Deep enough to worry me.

At first, I understood. I was pretty curious myself. I couldn't get the image of that dude in the lead truck out of my head. Confident, cool and cradling that AR-15.

You see this guy?

Turns out the Oregon militia was actively recruiting members and – surprise, surprise – held monthly public meetings like the friggin' PTA. When Sean discovered that the group's next gathering was in February, just two weeks away, he practically begged me to go with him.

"Let's check it out. It'll be fun."

"No way," I said. "Those guys are Loony Tunes."

Sean just chuckled. "Maybe. Let's see."

The meeting was to be held in a flyspeck town about three hours east called Crestview, known mostly for marionberry pie and Amish-style furniture. Also, diehard Republicans and conspiracy theorists. And gun enthusiasts, of course. They gathered in a large room inside the local fire station, which seemed odd given the taxpayer funding.

I warned Sean about the drive time, but he wasn't deterred.

"Free entertainment, dude," he reasoned, tousling his bushy blond hair. "I'll add more songs to my playlist. Put a coupla scooby doobies in the glove box. We'll be good to go."

It's always been hard saying no to Sean. Especially when he gives me that mischievous grin. The one that lights up his hazel eyes, making the freckles on his pale face stand out.

At first, I thought Sean might be fantasizing about being a militia man in order to impress women. I saw how he lingered on the True Patriots website, salivating over the uniforms with their customized shoulder patches, the T-shirts and bumper stickers available for purchase.

"We're not signing up just so you can get laid," I told him, only half joking.

But then I saw Sean freeze like a bird dog when he came across a recent photo of the commander. He was in military-style gear head to toe, including hard-knuckled gloves and combat boots. A sidearm was holstered off his right hip, a long knife strapped to his left thigh.

Terrifying. And yet in the picture he's standing casually on a Crestview street corner across from Daisy's Pancake House. Like it's totally normal.

"What's his name?" I ask Sean.

"He goes by Viper. All the militia dudes have these cool code names."

This is trouble, I'm thinking. Straight out of COD, Sean's wheelhouse. I search for a way to quickly break him out of it. My go-to in such situations is humor.

"Great. I'll call you Burrito Supreme," I say, straight-faced.

"You're Extra Cheese Pie."

"Roger that, BS."

"That's a hard copy, Pie."

We both laugh. I have less success steering him away from the laptop, closing the door to a disturbing alternate universe.

"Up for some God of War?"

"Nah, gonna keep reading for a while, I think."

"Okay, pal."

I leave the room with a knot in my gut. It's not like Sean to pass on a chance to slay a club-wielding troll. But maybe I just need to chill a little.

What's the harm in looking?

———

We didn't become friends in a normal way.

Actually, we started out as enemies – combatants in an epic dirt clod battle.

It was mid-August and I was 9, craving some semblance of excitement. School was still a coupla weeks off, and all the summer camps and sports leagues were done for the season.

There was an area a few blocks from my home being cleared for further development, and the dozers and backhoes had unearthed a few arrowheads and leafy fossils, drawing the interest of local kids, myself included. But on this particular afternoon, there were no new artifacts to be found.

The curse of late-summer boredom seemed unbreakable.

The construction site was deserted for the weekend, so I grabbed a baseball-sized clod and threw it at the side of a snoozing yellow backhoe. It exploded on impact, creating a small dust cloud. If only the machine could return fire, I thought.

Moments later, I spotted a boy my age absently drawing circles with a stick at the bottom of the slope, looking just as bored as I was. From a distance, the circles resembled targets. Why waste them? I held the strategic advantage of high ground, after all.

I quickly scooped some choice soil bombs into a pile. Then I let one fly in a high arc.

It burst dramatically at the kid's feet, prompting him to spin around, searching for the culprit. He didn't see me right away, which was disappointing. So, I announced myself.

"Hey, jerk-face!"

The boy squared his body in my direction, a tactical mistake. I hit him in the chest with a second clump, leaving a lovely chocolate-colored mark on his white hoodie.

Without hesitation, he snatched a clod of his own and fired back. It soared over my head, making me duck.

Giggling with newfound joy, I plucked another grenade from my arsenal, but before I could straighten, a clod spanked me hard in the butt, leaving a large brown stain.

"Har! You crapped your pants!" the boy yelled.

The battle raged until it was nearly dark and we were both exhausted. We declared a cease fire and the pale-faced boy scrambled up the hill to introduce himself.

"I'm Sean," he said with a gap-toothed grin. "Next time, I'm here and you're down there."

We were both claiming victory and laughing when my older sister stomped over in a huff to summon me to supper. She looked at Sean and me, covered head to sneaker in dirt and sweat, and rolled her eyes as only a 15-year-old can.

"Idiots."

Thus ended our very cool, very brief war.

The next day, my dad decided on a whim to embark on an end-of-summer family camping trip, so I didn't see Sean again until the first day of school. He was in my third-grade class, looking anxious. We were both new to the neighborhood and Pritchard Elementary, which gave us something to bond over, I suppose.

We began hanging out, sharing a passion for miniature plastic army men. We'd build forts for them out of dominos and Legos, then wage intricate battles fueled by our imagination. We'd also trade comic books and hone our reading skills by play-acting the best action scenes, aided by various homemade props and costumes. I was Spider-Man; he favored Batman. We couldn't wait to get home from school.

He always came to my house to play, but I never thought anything of it until my mom told me one day that she wanted to invite Sean's parents over for dinner.

When I brought it up, Sean's face went blank, as if stricken by a blown fuse.

"Don't think so," he said quietly. "My mom is super busy, working two jobs and all. And I don't really have a dad."

"Whaddya mean?"

"He left when I was three. I don't even remember his face, and there aren't any pictures in the house. Only blank spaces in photo albums."

My heart went out to Sean after that.

It had to be tough for him growing up, feeling abandoned, but he never complained or felt sorry for himself. He had a gentle soul and was kind almost to a fault, tearing up one day when I swatted a Daddy Long Legs with a rolled-up magazine and fretting whenever I got into a snit with one of my obnoxious siblings. Which was fairly often.

My father went out of his way to help fill Sean's parental void, patiently teaching him basic do-it-yourself skills in our garage and inviting him to come along on our camping trips. It was Sean's responsibility to help me set up the tent, and mom and dad lavishly praised Sean for his efforts.

"That's a fine job, son," my dad would say, making Sean glow.

He was goofy and lazy in an endearing way, and his later pursuit of the perfect strain of cannabis only cemented that image. He never seemed to take anything seriously, including the frustrated girls he dated, but I knew, deep inside, there was another Sean. One he rarely let others see.

I saw it for the first time when we were freshmen in high school. That's when he took a bullet for me. Well, not literally. But he did save my life.

We were kicking back with Mountain Dews after doing some bashing and crashing in Grand Theft Auto. The local news came on with a story about a shipwreck being discovered. Major chunks of a 300-year-old Spanish galleon had surfaced inside an ocean cave about 20 miles away due to some unusual, swirling tides.

It was my idea to get off the couch and check it out – maybe snag us a solid gold souvenir or two – before the wreck was hauled off to some museum or claimed by the National Park Service.

Neither of us had cars and it happened to be snowing, a relatively rare event on the North Coast. But we didn't let that stop us.

Sean "borrowed" his mother's Mazda and we drove as far as we could. Then, in the middle of winter, we began scaling a windswept, rocky cliff above the cave because I thought I'd spotted a way to climb down.

The trail quickly narrowed to a ledge that was only inches wide and freshly frosted with ice. I remember Sean looking at me and laughing. "We're mountain goats!" he said.

But we kept going.

We didn't care that it was treacherous. We were young and invincible – and there was treasure to be had. I led Sean along the face of the cliff. We were nearly at a point where we could start our descent when one of my sneakers slipped, twisting my body.

My fingers lost their grip on the slick rock and I found myself plunging toward the icy water about 25 feet below. I remember the splash and the pain of slamming sideways into an underwater boulder.

I came to in a hospital bed with my head wrapped in bandages. They told me I had a concussion and some bad bruises, but was otherwise okay.

Sean, though, was in intensive care suffering from severe hypothermia.

At the cliff, he had stripped down to his T-shirt and boxers. He dove in after me, somehow managing to pull me onto a large rock shelf near the entrance to the cave. Then he peeled off my wet clothes and dressed me in his discarded sweatpants and flannel shirt.

A couple of hours later, he flagged down a kayaker who had the same interest in seeing the shipwreck, only in a safe way. The man used his cellphone to alert the Coast Guard.

Fortunately for us, the Coasties came quickly. The incident report stated that Sean was "in and out of consciousness" and mumbling incoherently about goats.

So, that's it. The story of my greatest debt.

CHAPTER
THREE
ALEX

THERE'S COLD SWEAT on my water bottle. I absently draw a line with my index finger as Henderson drones on about Republicans.

Always Republicans.

We're in my office deep in the Capitol. The one decorated with child art like a classroom. Past my window the sun is sinking, creating a luminous entanglement of yellow, magenta and cyan. A Maxfield Parrish masterpiece.

Thinking of art always makes me think of her. I feel trapped behind this big desk when I should be sharing a sweet embrace. I grasp the bottle and it's smooth like her thighs and that draws a sigh.

Henderson doesn't appear to notice. His words are fuzzy, lost on the edges of my lustful daydream, but I can see his mouth opening and closing like a beached fish.

There's one member of my staff who knows about her, and it's not Harry Henderson, a veteran political strategist who runs his own polling firm and whose salary, as of 26 days ago, is being paid for by the Democratic National Committee. They called him a "visionary" and "genius," but I find him self-absorbed and abrasive.

Not everything can be reduced to poll numbers. Sometimes it's just right and wrong. Moral and immoral. Sometimes the polling can go to hell.

I twist the simple gold band that could be my wedding ring, only it's on the wrong finger. It always brings the world back into focus, leaving me feeling hollow.

"They're mobilizing. We have to get out ahead of it, senator."

I'm sunk deep into my leather chair. I look up at Henderson, see him bent over an arm's length away, lasering me with those beady eyes. His bald head is shining with perspiration.

"What does Wes say?" I ask, a little too loudly. It's more a call for help than a question.

Henderson is about to pontificate some more when Westley Matthews, my chief of staff, mercifully materializes.

"We'll circle back on this later, Harry," he says, giving the pudgy pollster a gentle shove toward the door.

"Tomorrow morning, first thing," Henderson says, scowling. "It's vitally important."

"Absolutely. Tomorrow."

Rebuffed, Henderson stomps off in the direction of his cubicle, where he's set up a miniature computer lab, including two Apple laptops filled with spreadsheets and fever charts that he feeds constantly like a brood of miniature schnauzers.

Wes gives me his familiar lopsided grin, the one weighted down by not-so-veiled sarcasm.

"News flash: The far right hates your gun bill. Boy, he seemed worked up. What was he talking about?"

I shake my head. "No clue, I tuned him out."

"I'll talk to him, Alex. He's a tad intense, but he does have your back. His sources in both parties are good. They can be valuable down the stretch."

"Yeah, I get it. We can't let this bill fail like all the others."

"We're still a few votes short, but after your next big speech maybe some minds will be swayed. Henderson says four senators are on the fence, all Republicans."

Even after all the massacres. Even after Marsten. All that blood spilled. All those innocent children. What will it take?

"I'll give it my best."

"I know you will. You always do."

Wes has been busy setting up a televised town hall-style meeting in Oregon that he hopes will sway some of my undecided colleagues. He wanted to do it in Portland, but I picked Astoria. Her town.

"How's that event coming along?" I ask.

"Looking good. CNN and MSNBC are going live. AP, Reuters and a dozen or so reporters will be there. I hired a local freelancer to help with the PR."

"What about our friends at Fox?"

Wes cocks an eyebrow, adding another layer to his derision. The talking heads at Fox had been excoriating my gun control bill for weeks now. A veritable gang bang. One of them had even suggested that I was a pawn of the Chinese Communist Party in a secret plot to weaken America. That, naturally, had further riled up a Republican base that was already foaming at the mouth.

"Believe it or not, I couldn't get a definitive answer."

"And the other ... *matter?*"

His whiskered face fills with concern. "All set as well. You sure about that? If news leaked now, when we're so close ..."

I don't pull rank. I seldom do. I simply turn away, back to the sunset.

It's been too long. I have to see her, feel whole if only for a night.

"I'm sure," I say and close my eyes, hoping to see her face.

———

The hardest thing about being a survivor of a school shooting is the guilt.

Not the guilt of surviving while others died. It's the guilt of not doing more when the bullets rip and the bodies fall. The guilt that persists even when, in the horrible days to follow, they proclaim you a hero.

There's always more you could have done. So much more. A torrent of self-blame. Why couldn't you have reacted faster? Why didn't you barricade the classroom door? Club him as he barged in? Why couldn't you come up with his name, reason with him, stop the madness?

Two years have passed now and still there is grief. It clings like a lacquer that can't be thinned or sanded off, but it's also fuel. Very powerful fuel. There's that at least.

Two of my fellow survivors couldn't withstand the memory of carnage. The nightmares that followed. The haunting spawned by such close proximity to evil.

They took their own lives in the weeks that followed. A fellow teacher and the vice principal, a cheery woman named Sandra who had failed to press the button under her desk in her panic. Nobody mentioned the dark irony of her using a firearm to commit suicide in the wake of a shooting rampage.

Becky, a second-grade teacher and newly minted grandmother

who shared her homemade pies and tarts with us in the faculty lounge, drove off a rocky cliff on the ocean highway south of Cannon Beach. When first responders found her crumpled Volvo, she was still alive. "Let me die," she pleaded. Her wish was granted halfway to the hospital.

I read the news with sadness, but I also understood.

In my sleep I see the innocent faces of two children entrusted to me as they took their last breaths. The bewilderment in their eyes as their lives drained away, the mounting fear as a young man with peach fuzz cheeks calmly reloaded his assault rifle in the middle of their sixth-grade classroom. *My classroom.*

It's my fuel and also my curse.

It was an ordinary morning in February, damp and nearly freezing. The boiler in the basement of McReedy Elementary School was groaning, straining to produce enough heat.

All 16 of my kids showed up, a small fact that I remember because it was winter and a flu bug was going around Marsten, our friendly little river town – one of the few in the state that could still boast employment through both commercial fishing and logging. The local paper mill employed 450, just down from its peak of 520 in the early '90s.

The motto carved into the welcome sign is "A Caring Community," and it's mostly true. We care about each other. Even when the smoking barrel of a gun turns our way. Even then.

We thought we were prepared. Staff members and children had practiced "active shooter" drills. An emergency buzzer had been installed in the office, linked directly to the sheriff's office so nobody had to take precious seconds to call 911. We added security cameras, inside and out. We even formed a standing committee to evaluate our readiness and recommend improvements. I volunteered to serve. It was my idea to bring in a security expert who was a combat vet, a friend of a friend.

He showed up in fatigues and a crewcut under an Army cap, lending himself a certain gravitas. His advice was taken seriously, and he led a drill or two, but he couldn't prepare us for the terror and the speed at which it unfolded. The paralysis of nerves. The desire to drop and curl into a fetal position. The lightning stroke that tells your brain to run like hell even if you have to knock people out of the way.

We were hardly the first. Newtown, Parkland, Columbine, Uvalde … there had been many other massacres inside schools at the hands of deranged gunmen, the kind that prey on the most vulnerable. The most innocent. Some acted out of a twisted desire for revenge after being bullied or slighted, others wrote screeds soaked in narrow-minded, racist beliefs. Most were simply psychotic weirdos. They all had one thing in common – a lust for weapons that would make them feel all-powerful. I forced myself to read up on the shootings, hoping to learn from the past in order to help protect my school.

We were all warned, and yet when it happened to us warnings weren't nearly enough. The grim scenes play over and over in my mind.

Twelve-year-old Greta Thorne is reading her essay on the Founding Fathers to the class when I hear the first pops. Then the piercing screams, followed by breaking glass and splintering wood.

I rise from my desk, blinking stupidly for a few seconds as my brain processes the sensory data. The children all turn to me – the adult in the room.

Heavy boots thump in the hall, moving closer.

There's the sound of an ammo clip being inserted, then a booming barrage of gunfire as he shreds Mrs. Carson's classroom – the one directly across the hall. I hear her plead "They're children!" only to be greeted with a second burst.

There's no escape route. The hall is a killing zone. The windows are blocked by fish tanks, books and art projects. There's no time.

"The closet! Everyone in the closet!"

Boys and girls run to me as I open the door to the supply closet. A dozen are huddled inside on the floor as the shooter opens my door. I'm shepherding the others, practically shoving them in, when I turn and see the face of the man with the gun.

"They all have to die," he says with eerie certainty. "You, too."

I remember thinking he's just a kid himself, with long, stringy brown hair, acne and a patchy mustache that looked as if sparrows had been pecking at it. He's wearing a flannel shirt, jeans and hiking boots with untied laces.

I thought I'd seen him somewhere before. Not in my class, but somewhere in town.

"Wait, I know you," I say.

He pauses, rocks back on his heels. Only two children remain outside the closet now.

"No, you don't. You're one of *them.*"

"I can help you. Just ... put down the gun. We can talk."

"Sorry, too late."

He squeezes the trigger of the Bushmaster XM-15, putting a bullet in my side.

The second slug tears into Teddy Paulson, the boy I'd been trying to shield with my body. Greta, inches to my right, looks at me in fright as she's shot. Then again.

I slump over their bloody, mutilated bodies, certain I would die. But not before I close the closet door with my hip.

As I lose consciousness, I feel him trying to move me out of the way. Pulling on my legs. I can hear tiny cries from behind the door.

And then nothing.

They tell me at the hospital that deputies took the gunman out as he was aiming at my kids in the closet. They say I saved their lives, bought them invaluable seconds.

"How many?" I ask in a hoarse whisper, and the sheriff knew I was talking about lives lost.

"Twenty-eight," Butch Simpson says, removing his sheriff's office ball cap as if he was standing at the side of a freshly dug grave instead of my bed. "Four adults, the rest children. Never seen anything like it. Modified assault rifle, magazines duct-taped together for speedier reload. We found 300 rounds in his backpack. He would have taken out every living soul."

I swallow hard, trying to comprehend the insanity. "Is there a reason?"

"Not that we've found so far. He painted **UVALDE** on the barrel. He'd been planning this for a while."

"Thought I recognized him."

"Possibly. Bobby Allen Crane. Local boy. Parents own a fishing boat and restaurant. Diagnosed bi-polar, the family says. And yet they let him build an arsenal. We pulled a dozen guns out of his trailer. He just turned 18. Bought the Bushmaster two weeks ago, using his dad's credit card."

"Jesus."

"I think Jesus took the day off yesterday. It's all so … *terrible*."

Simpson struggles to maintain his composure. He'd always seemed so ruggedly unflappable. A stoic Marlboro Man with a badge. Now, standing there, he seems as fragile as bone china – one more emotional blow from falling apart.

"Principal Harris?"

"Gone."

I shake my head and wince. Any movement hurts, even with the painkillers.

The principal had just announced that he'd be retiring at the end of the school year. He had been a friend and a mentor, telling me he'd recommend me as his replacement to the school board. I didn't have the heart to tell him I didn't want the job. I wasn't planning to stay that long.

The supervising nurse steps in the room and instructs Simpson to let me rest. Reminds him I'm on potent medicine for a reason.

"Sorry, Alex," the lawman says, putting his cap back on. "They tell me you're lucky. The bullet went straight through, missing major organs. When you're ready, the investigators will want a statement. I'll come see you after you're discharged."

"That would be nice."

Tears are streaming down my cheeks now. The sheriff's own eyes are red and watery.

"If you hadn't stalled him … if you hadn't laid your body down, he'd have killed them all," he says. "I want you to know that."

I close my eyes, let the drugs do their thing. The first of the nightmares soon follows.

———

Three days later, I spoke at Greta's funeral.

I rose from my wheelchair and gripped the lectern and people applauded. Through tears, I remembered my bright-eyed student, her chestnut hair in braids. Just 12 and so full of promise. My best student.

I rolled into the funeral home with no prepared remarks. I couldn't focus enough to write anything down, but I felt a yearning to pay my respects to the Thorne family.

The reporters who were there wrote that I talked "passionately and powerfully" for more than 20 minutes. They said I went on to condemn the gun lobby, chastise the Washington establishment for failing to address the senseless violence sweeping the country and vow to take action that would "wake up" America.

Honestly, I remember none of that. Not the words, not the ovation afterward. I had to watch the video later and when I did it surprised me. It seemed like another person, or perhaps just a new me, reborn in the fire of unspeakable horror.

I'm no radical. Not even now, despite what the conservatives in D.C. say about me. At the time of the McReedy massacre, I was a single woman in her 30s, a grade school teacher for six years who was working nights on a master's in education with plans to one day move into a principal's office. Not exactly grand ambitions.

I was seeing a woman named Mandy Malone and we were in love, but we kept it quiet. We feared the repercussions, the dirty looks, the recriminations. Some likely spoken in anger, more muttered behind our backs. A lesbian teaching our children? *Influencing them?* Intolerance is one of the drawbacks of life in a small town that rarely makes the pro/con list. There's a fear of change in rural America and it's palpable.

She wanted to move to San Francisco, where people were more

open-minded. Where she didn't have to pretend she was straight. Where we could kiss in public and hold hands like other couples. Get married. Start a family through science or adoption.

I told her yes and began applying for teaching jobs in the Bay Area. I was already working on my thesis. Besides, I thought a change of scenery might be nice.

The shooting changed everything. A screwed-up teenager with a gun changed the trajectory of my life as nothing else could.

It started with a community "healing" – a prayerful outdoor event held two weeks after the bloodshed led by a local pastor. I came to pay tribute to the victims at what had become an impromptu memorial, a length of chain-link fence facing the playground. By then, scores of flower bouquets and stuffed bears had been woven into the links, along with handwritten messages of love and anguish rolled up like tiny scrolls. Our very own wailing wall.

Afterward, I spoke to some of the victims' families and a plan began to take form. We wouldn't accept the violence as a fact of life. We wouldn't merely lament what had happened. We'd shake things up, starting with a novel lawsuit against the Longview, Washington, store that sold the Bushmaster, the young gunman's parents and the company that built a weapon designed to kill and maim people.

We knew it was a long shot. We knew it was likely to fail. And yet we all agreed to try. A strong message had to be sent.

Fortunately for us, Mandy's father was a lawyer and not just any lawyer, but a damn good one. He had retired from corporate law on the East Coast and moved the family to Bend, where he ran a hobby ranch with a couple of horses and six cows and did high-priced consulting on the side. Michael Malone took our case for free, regretting only that he didn't come up with the idea first.

I'm not exactly sure how I became the spokeswoman for our group. It may have been my viral eulogy or passionate desire to achieve lasting change on behalf of the victims. I certainly didn't seek the burden of talking to reporters and news anchors, of explaining the lawsuit to the people of Marsten, many of whom are fervent defenders of the Second Amendment. But in the wake of the shooting, they *listened*. And that gave me hope.

After the first dozen interviews, it became easier. I had memorized the key talking points, loaded in enough sound bites for the evening news. My jitters at appearing live on national TV subsided after a while. Mandy told me I looked "comfortable" on camera.

For the biggest interviews, Malone sat beside me. He'd handle the legal questions so I could focus on the shooting and its toll. We made a good team. If only our results were as good as our passion.

Judges stripped defendants from our suit like orange peels and after six months of briefs and arguments we were forced to admit defeat. On appeal, even the gun manufacturer was dismissed. The gun store closed its doors rather than risk a major payout. A tiny victory, but not nearly enough.

That's when Wes came to my door.

Mandy was in Seattle at a friend's sculpture unveiling. I was alone, exhausted from all the media attention. I practically cheered when the last satellite TV truck rumbled out of town, bound for the next disaster.

———

I'm lying on the sofa with classic blues and beer for company, feeling defeated.

33

There are three loud knocks and I freeze, hoping whoever it is goes away. But he hears the music and knocks again, only louder.

"Ms. Austin?" a deep voice says from the other side. "I'm not a reporter."

Groaning, I get up. Cracking the door, I see an earnest face peering at me. He's thin with a shadow of a beard, about 6-foot-2 in a blue suit, slightly rumpled. His striped tie is askew and there are flecks of dirt on his black shoes. The dirt intrigues me for some inexplicable reason.

Where has he been?

"Westley Matthews," he says, extending an arm. "I'm a political consultant over in Portland. Can we talk?"

I sigh and shake his hand, then wave him in. He accepts my offer of a beer and takes a big gulp before sitting down in the antique armchair directly in front of me, a reupholstered inheritance from my grandmother. He perches on the edge of the cushion like someone about to take a dive.

"Look, I don't want to be rude, but I'm wiped out," I say, turning down the volume of a woeful guitar solo with the app on my phone. "Let's make it brief, okay?"

"You got it. I've seen all your interviews over the past few days. Exhausting, I'm sure."

"What brings you to the metropolis of Marsten, Westley?"

"I like that – how you cut to the chase. Please, call me Wes."

I pick up my beer but it's empty and I'm too tired to go back to the fridge. My irritation only grows.

Wes inches closer and I begin to fear that he will fall off his chair and smack his head on my glass coffee table.

"Have you given any thought to taking your gun control fight to another level?"

"Um, we just lost, in case you didn't notice," I say, regretting the bitterness lacing my words.

"Of course you did. But you must have known that going in – that your lawsuit was more a statement than a means of real change. The courts aren't going to reform gun laws. The people must, through the representatives they elect."

"Ah, I see. So you're going to offer me some secret recipe for turning the tide in Washington? Please, please do."

Wes laughs off my sarcasm and finally leans back.

"The only way to take on the gun lobby is from the inside. But only if you're a true champion."

"What are you saying?"

"I'm saying you need to run for office."

"I'm no politician."

"That will work in your favor in this state, believe me. People are sick and tired of career politicians. But you, on the other hand, are fiercely independent, a smart-as-a-whip educator turned advocate, and a hero to boot."

"Good Lord, please stop. I'm no hero. I'm a survivor. And I have zero interest in being governor."

"I couldn't agree more. You should set your sights higher: United States Senate."

It's my turn to laugh. "Is this some kind of joke? I couldn't possibly win. Russell Riley is an institution in Oregon. He's beloved."

"Maybe once upon a time. Now he's old and out of touch. He'll be 78 next year. He gets out of breath walking a flight of stairs and refuses to Tweet. In the last election, a Libertarian got 18 percent of the vote. *A Libertarian!* Imagine what a dynamic, youthful person such as yourself could do."

This is ridiculous. Utter nonsense. I don't have time for this, but he seems clever and I can't resist sounding him out some more.

"Wouldn't it be smarter to wait until he retires? Why take on a fellow Democrat like that?"

"Because the party will field a candidate and it will be more of the same. Another moderate unwilling to take risks. This is our best chance, maybe in 50 years, if you're truly serious about gun control. We can build a coalition and take Riley down. Surprise the SOB. He'll be too cocksure of himself to take you seriously – until it's too late."

I can feel his energy filling the room. It seeps into my soul, lifting my spirits.

"Who the hell are you?" I ask.

"The man who will manage your campaign," he says with a lopsided grin. "If you'll have me."

CHAPTER
FOUR
ALEX

THE FIRST POLLS showed me trailing the incumbent by more than 25 points. I was neck-and-neck with a DJ-rapper who called himself Soul2Man.

It seemed like an epic mismatch. Riley started the primary campaign with $20 million in reserve and a series of major fundraisers lined up in D.C. and the vital Portland metro area. I had a war chest of $6,342.

Wes told me not to worry.

"We're lulling him to sleep," he said, smirking.

We spent weeks together refining our message, creating a platform that would resonate with Oregonians still stunned by the Marsten bloodshed.

It was Wes' idea to draft a list of "priorities" that could win us votes, such as protecting forests and rivers and preventing wildfires. Such as getting the homeless into more shelters and treatment programs and off city streets. Such as boosting tourism in regions where lumber mills and fish canneries had been shuttered.

But the centerpiece of the campaign would be a multipronged

plan to curb gun violence in America.

It was wildly ambitious and tricky, requiring us to weave a path through a gauntlet of interest groups. Wes turned out to be quite adept at that, booking me on various TV and internet programs. The message slowly began picking up steam, reverberating with families who wanted nothing more than to keep their kids safe.

Three months before the May primary, we'd cut the deficit to 10 points. Liberal gun control groups around the country began sensing a rare opportunity. Money began rolling in, enabling us to do our first mailers and 30-second TV spots. Soul2Man dropped out, endorsing me. At least I would get the rapper vote.

But victory still seemed a remote possibility. The West Coast reporters kept reminding me of that, asking if I was "really serious" or "just seeking publicity."

They stopped asking after my one and only debate with Riley. As the underdog, we'd proposed a series of six. His camp agreed to one.

"They're foolish to debate you at all," Wes told me. "You'll make mincemeat out of him. You've blossomed into a formidable candidate."

He was right – about the mincemeat. At the televised debate at the University of Oregon in Eugene, I was on my game. He wasn't. I left him shell-shocked and stammering.

Afterward, Wes and I were celebrating at a bar, sipping margaritas. But the good vibe didn't last long.

"I don't know how to say this," he begins. "Please don't hate me for it."

"Oh God, just spit it out."

"Your personal life … it can hurt us."

"What? Are you talking about Mandy? I love her."

"I know, I know. And it would be one thing if you two were already out there, but you're not. Nobody knows, even the good people of Marsten. You've kept it a secret. I can understand why, I really can – but now it hurts us."

"Fuck you. My personal life is off-limits. You know that."

"Alex, please. Riley's people are out looking for dirt. The Republicans, too. They'll hurt you any way they can. You need to be aware of that. I'm only doing my job. Honest."

I'm incensed, but Wes hasn't steered me wrong yet. I need to hear him out.

"Go ahead."

"I think it's best that you and Mandy stay apart for a while – just until after the election. A sabbatical of sorts. Then we can figure out a way to make your relationship public, but on our terms. Do it the right way. There's been openly gay couples in politics. The trick is to own it."

"So, it's a *trick* to you?"

"That's not what I'm saying," he says, looking wounded. "Look, I'm trying to help you."

"Tammy Baldwin broke that barrier years ago."

"Yes, but Tammy came out long before she ran for the Senate. She was totally upfront about it. It's a big difference. Look, you two can get married on live TV if you want to, just not now, when we're so close. I'm sorry, this is hard for me to say."

Is this really happening?

"Mandy and I can do an interview with one of the more enlightened journalists," I say, sounding desperate. "That woman from Vanity Fair was nice, I thought. I think she knew."

Wes shakes his head. "You're not hearing me. It's too close to the election. It'll boomerang on us. The other side will accuse you of hiding the truth from the voters. There will be rampant speculation about what else you're not revealing. It's not a good look. Not when we're only trailing by 4 points and closing the gap by the day. Do the magazine interview after we win. That's a good idea."

"I hate this. It's like we're going back in time. Believe it or not, I went into politics to be my true self – to make a difference."

"I know. I hate saying any of this out loud. But, Alex, if you win you'll be the greatest champion of gun safety this country has ever had. I have zero doubt about that."

I'm no politician, but already compromises are enveloping me, stealing my breath like pythons. I finish my drink and rise to my feet. I take a few seconds to glower at the pained man at the table.

"If I lose her over this," I say, "I'll never forgive you."

——

We won the primary by a hair – less than 10,000 votes.

Riley graciously conceded rather than demand a recount, thanking me later for greasing his path to retirement and a luxury condo on a San Diego golf course after 32 years in office.

Oregon Democrats and open-minded independents propelled me to a double-digit victory in November over a gaffe-prone Republican former state rep who thought climate change was a hoax and that "99 percent" of immigrants were violent criminals.

But I lost anyway. I lost her.

Mandy wasn't in the hall in Portland when I gave my victory speech and thanked my supporters. She didn't move with me to Washington. She did exactly what I asked. She stayed away.

The distance between us was more than miles.

My calls and emails increasingly went unanswered. My emotional texts would elicit one-word replies. I'd never felt so lost, so adrift. At a gun violence conference, I suddenly burst into tears. The people at my table thought I was just being passionate about my top issue. I was thinking about Mandy.

I consoled myself by drowning in paperwork – the detritus of politics – drafting and re-drafting my gun bill. But I never stopped thinking of her.

I visited when she allowed it, but it was always a clandestine affair orchestrated by Wes with a knowing wink by my security team. Mandy resented all of it, but topping the list was my lack of courage. The "hero" of the school shooting was really an emotional coward, unable to reveal herself and stand by the woman she loves. I hated myself for it.

In my absence, she made major changes. She came out, hanging rainbow bunting in the front window of her downtown Astoria gallery. She told me one day that she'd begun dating other women. I burst into tears and begged her to forgive me, falling to my knees on the burgundy shag rug in her living room.

"I love you! I love you!"

Mandy kissed my forehead and whispered, "That's not enough."

"Don't leave me," I pleaded.

"You left *me*, remember? So you can change the world? So, go change the world, just leave me out of it."

That was the last time I saw her.

I called later to tell her I'd be back in a few weeks. Told her I was planning to have a live TV forum on my bill at the Liberty Theatre, a short walk from her gallery.

Now, at last, I'm going to see her. I have no idea what she'll say and that terrifies me, but she's willing to allow me in and that's a start. I can't live without her any longer.

Wes doesn't know that. I love him like a brother, but I'm done taking his advice about my private life.

From now on, I go with my conscience and my heart, no matter how many conservatives are appalled.

No matter what the poll numbers say.

CHAPTER
FIVE
ROBB

EVERY DAY IS garbage day for Sean and his noisy white truck. For me, it's Tuesday morning around 7. That's when I find out what my people are up to. A little glimpse.

I have to roll those hulking trash and recycling bins from the side of the building to the curb, sometimes squeezing them between parked cars.

There are two red bins for recycling stuff like cardboard and plastic, a smaller blue bin for glass, and then there's another giant black bin just for trash. There's also a big green one for yard waste, but there's only a patch of shrubbery in front of the River Vista and concrete and gravel everywhere else, so it's rarely filled.

The rest are overflowing. I usually have to cram crap into the bins, rearranging a bit. It can be a little nasty, especially with the overstuffed trash bags. But the discarded boxes and bags always tell a story.

For instance, Aliston Sinclair, best described as an aspiring author and day trader, just bought a new computer monitor. He lives across the lobby from Sean and me. Kinda eccentric – the moody-when-sober type.

I see that Layla got some new paint named Midnight Stone. Sounds right up her alley. Dark and mysterious.

Christie Lopez, our Tik Tok influencer and beertender, had the usual fashion deliveries. Designer sandals. A pleated skirt. A floral scarf. She gets the overpriced clothes for free, just for mentioning it on her blog. Where does she put it all, I wonder? She's got a one-bedroom across from Mrs. Wong.

As for Mrs. Wong, I know almost everything she has delivered – and it's a crazy long list – because I have to lug it upstairs for her, along with endless piles of product catalogues in English and Chinese that she reads with a sliding magnifying glass. But she's okay. Just lonely, and always making me ramen soup. Best I've ever had.

I'm not a snoop. It's just in my face every Tuesday. The people in my building are pretty cool, and there isn't a lot of turnover, even though Aliston keeps telling me how he's about to strike it rich with some bestseller or computer algorithm for trading stocks or whatever.

I affectionately call my neighbors Mole People because whenever I'm in the halls doing my cleaning, or just going up to see Layla, they all pop their heads out. Every single time.

"Oh, it's you, Robb," they say as if surprised, and then disappear. Like Whac-a-Mole. You know, the old arcade game. Plastic moles pop randomly out of holes and you clobber them with a cartoonish, oversized mallet to score points.

The building is owned by Mrs. Wong's younger sister, who's in her late 70s and rich.

Chau Wong is a local real estate broker who specializes in big commercial properties. She's also a major landlord in town. Besides River Vista, she and her husband own four other downtown apartment buildings. I guess that's why people keep asking her to run for mayor. She turns them down, though. Too busy, she tells them. To me, she says, "People in Astoria would never elect a Chinese mayor." I hope that's not true.

I run into her at least once a week because she's always checking on her sister Luen. I try not to smell too much like pot when Chau's visiting because I know she disapproves, even though Oregon legalized weed years ago, one of the first states in the country. Still, I've been working for her for a while now and she's giving me a sweet discount on the rent plus $500 a month, so I try to act more or less professional when she's around.

On a recent Tuesday morning after putting the bins out, I'm heading up the front steps to the lobby, when I nearly get bowled over by Aliston, who's putting on his coat as he's dashing out the front door.

"Oops, sorry Robb. Big day," he says. "Very big day!"

"What's going on?" I shout after him, but he's already at the sidewalk, moving fast.

I wonder what he's up to. He has so many different jobs, with business cards for each. Besides his obsession with day trading in general and Amazon stock in particular, he teaches a computer class at the college and does some PR work on the side. I make a mental note to talk to him later.

I'm resetting the lobby rug when I hear fast-approaching footsteps. I brace myself for impact but it's Layla, coming down the stairs in her usual rhythmic way. Almost skipping.

I want to ask her what she's painting with Midnight Stone but that would be a little creepy because there's really no good answer to "How did you know?" I'll just wait and see for myself.

"Anything in your place need maintaining?" I ask, grinning.

"Only me," she says. "But I'm off to coffee with Mandy."

"Have I met her?"

Layla frowns. "Yes, several times. She runs Bellissima, remember?"

"Oh yeah. Walk past it all the time."

Bellissima is a fancy gallery a few blocks from my shop. I've never felt dressed up enough to venture inside. I'd met the owner at a couple of parties thrown by Layla's artist friends. Seemed nice enough. In her early 30s, with shapely legs and red hair that makes her look a little like Jessica Chastain, only taller.

"Mandy sold one of my paintings," Layla gushes. "I'm so excited."

"Awesome. Which one?" "The shoreline in oil."

"The one with the rolling mist?"

"Waves, doof. She keeps asking me to do an exhibit," she says, looking away. "I don't know."

"You should. You're brilliant."

"That's why I keep you around. For the on-cue compliments."

"I'm the wind in your sails."

She groans. I ask if she wants to have a beer later.

"Call me," she says, sliding past close enough that I can smell the coconut from her shampoo. "Maybe try to be ever-so-slightly romantic?"

"*You? Romance?* Since when?"

"You can do it, Romeo. I'm not talking about flowers. If you bring me goddamn roses, I'll punch you in the nose. Bye!"

"Whew. For a minute there, I thought you'd changed."

I check my watch. I need to paint some seriously scuffed base moulding in the lobby before heading to Spoke & Wheel at noon. I grab a can and brush from the basement and am about halfway done with the work when I see the owner's silver Mercedes pull up in front.

The driver comes around to open the passenger door and out steps Chau – never one to act her age – decked out in a form-fitting striped dress and rose-tinted, cat-eye glasses.

I'm wearing my coveralls and a frayed Mariners cap dotted with paint drips of various shades, but I straighten as she glides in.

"Hello, darling," she says, eyeing my brush suspiciously. "Don't forget the 'wet paint' sign when you're finished."

"Will do." I notice the pink box dangling from her slender wrist. "Coffee cake?"

"Cookies. Luen's favorite: oatmeal-molasses. Robb, I have a small favor to ask."

"Sure, what's up?"

"My sister is getting carried away with her shopping. Everything goes on my Amex card, you see, so I'm well aware of her spending habits. I'm going to talk with her about it, but, in the meantime, if you could stop bringing up her catalogues I think that would help. Less temptation."

"But she loves looking at them."

"My sweet darling, if only that was all she did. She bought $8,000 worth of merchandise last month. A bedroom set, an inflatable Jacuzzi and a bamboo crib. Fortunately, I was able to cancel the orders before they arrived. I think she really just enjoys chatting with the sales people."

"Oh, no," I say, feeling a little sad for Mrs. Wong. I make a silent pledge to chat with her more often.

"Thanks for understanding."

The owner smiles and disappears up the stairs. I hear chatter in Chinese, then a door closing.

I finish my painting and set my mind on my next daily goal: figuring out what constitutes "slightly" romantic.

———

Layla isn't really hard to figure out. She just wants the man in her life to make an effort, not take her for granted.

Expressing my feelings isn't a problem. My large Jewish-Italian family taught me how to give and receive all the major emotions. Anything bottled up would be drained – usually in front of an audience. Hugs, tears, screams and laughter were the grist of our supper club, starting with the cooking and running through dessert.

No, my problem is being revealed as someone who's unworthy. That's my curse, trailing me like a lost dog.

After high school, I was ghosted by attractive girls who either had no interest in a serious relationship or just didn't see as me as someone to get serious with. Most of them were of the spring break variety, so I guess honestly expressing my affection as love came as something of a shock. They dumped me for someone they could just screw around with.

So, guess I'm a little scarred.

I want to tell Layla that I love her. I really do. I just freeze. The words become ice cubes in my mouth. It's tough when the woman of your dreams lives two floors away but you can't tell her that because you're afraid you'll scare her off. Maybe that's why the painting is in my closet. Maybe not. I'm not good at figuring myself out. That's something my drama-hungry family never taught me.

I call Layla, like she wanted.

"Hi, Babe."

"Robbie."

"Just seeing if you want to get together."

"That's it?"

"Excuse me?"

"That's all you've got?"

Oh shit, the romantic part.

Layla has a way of getting to the point, hard and fast, like a switchblade in the ribs, but, hey, I'm no fboy. I'm really in deep. I tell her what I'd been honestly thinking about all day.

"It would be cool if we could go to the roof and watch the sunset."

She'd never invited me up to the Nest before and I was burning with curiosity.

"Hmm. That's my secret spiritual place. Why should I allow a non-believer to intrude?"

"But I'm a believer – in *you*. And I have beer. Your favorite."

"Hazies?"

Layla liked a cloudy California IPA called Hazy Little Thing. I liked how it got her in the mood.

"Absolutely," I say. "Whatever my lady wants, she gets."

"*Ding! Ding!* We have a winner!"

Layla's coarse laugh cuts through the phone. "Come on up."

Minutes later, the door to No. 5 swings open. Layla is in a long, powder-blue sweater unbuttoned temptingly low, a short black skirt and high leather boots. Her hair is pulled back, exposing her neck. Pure Grade A cream.

She accepts the beer with a big smile, then looks around me. "What – no roses?"

"Sorry, I like my nose."

"I like it, too. And those blue eyes."

She leans in and gives me a kiss, lingering a bit.

"Let's watch that sunset," she says.

I follow like a teenager in heat. She takes me through her bedroom, which is in its usual state of inviting disarray. Jumbled sheets, partially open drawers, a lacy bra hanging on a chair, an open novel waiting patiently for the journey to resume. She pulls up the window, steps through onto the fire escape, then looks back.

"Are you stoned?"

"Of course not," I say, a bit wounded that she'd think I would show up high for a date.

"Just be careful on the ladder. It's a little tricky."

She ambles up like an acrobat. I struggle to maintain my footing on the narrow metal steps and make the mistake of looking down 3 ½ stories to the street.

When I reach the top, I'm amazed.

Layla has set up what looks like a fancy beach cabana, complete with a foam bed covered with pillows and blankets. She slips the beer into a cooler and clicks a switch. Naked bulbs strung overhead start to glow. Jazz spills out of a portable speaker.

"What do you think?"

"No way," I say, shaking my head. "I'm going to have to cite you for creating an illegal Airbnb on my roof."

Layla laughs and I give her a hug. "You've created an awesome refuge, Lay. Perfect for an artist."

She points at an empty easel and nods. "When it's not rainy or windy. Which, unfortunately, isn't as often as I'd like."

Taking my hand, she tugs me down to the bed. Suddenly we're side by side, gazing into each other's eyes. The sun is sinking fast, leaving blue and orange streaks in the sky. It looks like one of her paintings.

Layla's lips part and I bring her closer, kissing her hard. I feel her body shudder. I move to that impossibly smooth neck of hers as she unbuttons my denim shirt.

She moans softly as I squeeze her breasts, then guides me back to her lips. I feel her warm tongue, her talented fingers on my zipper.

"I need you inside me," she whispers.

Like some kind of magic act, our clothes vanish.

———

We're lying in the cabana, her head resting on my chest, which is still heaving a bit. I comb her hair with my fingers as a soulful sax caresses the cool night air.

"I had no idea you like jazz," I say. "It's kinda nice."

"There's a lot about me you don't know." She gives my nipple a soft kiss. "But that's how it's supposed to be. A mystery that reveals itself over time."

"I'm an open book, I'm afraid. No secrets, very little mystery."

"Oh, you have your secrets."

"No, really, I don't. Not with you, anyway."

"That's sweet," she says. "But I like surprises. I don't need to know everything. Just … the important things."

Layla gives me an odd, penetrating look. She sees the puzzled look on my face and ends the suspense with a heavy sigh.

"Sean told me you two have been looking into joining True Patriots," she says. She's gone from seductress to stern principal in 60 seconds. "He said you're into it. Doing a lot of research. Says you're both going to a meeting."

"Oh, *that*."

She frowns. "You're thinking about joining a violent extremist group and you don't think it's something I should know? Or are you just hiding it from me?"

I stroke her silky shoulder. "I would never hide anything from you, Babe. I'm just keeping an eye on Sean. Trying to keep him out of trouble."

"By going to one of their meetings like a couple of fanboys?"

"By revealing the truth about them. He's getting obsessed. You know Sean, it's the only way. The research I've done so far shows how dangerous they are. I'll present it to him – the plain facts – and he'll stop. Move on."

I hope.

"What did you find out?"

"A lot. The leader of True Patriots was booted out of the service for suspected crimes against civilians in Iraq. Now he's under investigation for attacking migrants at the border and making death threats against politicians who support gun control. He's bad news. I'm meeting with a former founding member who quit last year. He goes by the code name Talisman. Lives here in town. I'm sure he'll give me an earful."

"*Code name?* Are you kidding? Have you told Sean what you found?"

"Not yet. I need to nail it down some more first, otherwise he'll just poke holes." Layla shakes her head. "I can't believe he's getting sucked in. Militia people plotted to kidnap the Michigan governor over mask mandates, remember? They helped lead the insurrection at the Capitol."

"I know," I say. "Don't worry. I won't let them brainwash Sean."

"Or you."

"Especially me. Unless you'd like me in fatigues. Some women are turned on by men in …"

Layla gives me a pretend slap, grabs a couple of beers.

"I'm worried," she says, handing me one. "I shouldn't be, I guess. But I am."

The night is full of jazz, now with undertones of uncertainty.

I'm worried, too.

CHAPTER
SIX
ROBB

A SPELL HAD been cast over Sean.

The more he learned about True Patriots, the more excited he became. No matter how twisted their actions and beliefs seemed.

I quickly learned that in some parts of rural central and eastern Oregon, camo-clad disciples were revered. Sheriffs and police chiefs had formed an alliance with militia leaders, bending rules about public carry of firearms, while accepting the group's standing offer to assist as needed in major emergencies.

The alliance wasn't an uneasy one, like partnering with the Hells Angels. A number of militia members were local cops or ex-military, and they boasted about their allegiance on Facebook and Twitter.

But what really had me scratching my head was the whole service organization thing. Kind of a split personality.

The True Patriots' leader, Viper, had worked to foster a reputation for True Patriots as a patriotic Christian brotherhood that benefited the community.

Since militias in Oregon are technically illegal, TP was registered as a nonprofit – a social welfare organization formed on behalf of veterans.

Whether it was to further its cover or please its Marine founders, the militia did refer vets suffering from PTSD to therapists and offer occasional support groups. Members also volunteered to paint over gang graffiti and provided free firearms training. Officially, TP was non-partisan, just fiercely opposed to big government in all its forms. Especially any attempts at gun control.

On the Patriots website and in its chatrooms, racist and anti-Semitic rhetoric was kept to a low boil. The organization's guiding principles – available online – were written in such a way that conservative business people could climb aboard and not worry about a customer backlash.

Even the stickers, patches and belt buckles available for sale were deliberately low-key, each emblazoned with a "Don't Tread on Me" rattlesnake forming an oval with TP in the middle in red.

And yet, despite the efforts to seem, well, *normal*, a dark current ran through everything: The libs are coming for us with help from the "deep state," United Nations and ever-sinister Jewish bankers. The claims had a knowing urgency to them, like a biblical Noah warning about an approaching storm front.

"Judgment Day!" one militia member wrote in a post. "First, they'll take our guns. Then the rest of our freedoms. The time to resist is now!"

I found it chilling. For Sean, it was adult cosplay, only with real bullets.

The day of the meeting, I'd never seen him so pumped. On the drive over, I felt guilty that I was brainstorming ways to puncture his shiny new balloon.

We walk in a few minutes late with little idea what to expect. We had hoped it would be a room full of rugged military men, swapping war stories. It's nothing of the sort.

The audience is full of people on Medicare. Silver hair and canes. A wrinkled woman knitting something blue from the ball of yarn in her lap. The room is in the rear of the firehouse, so as not to interfere with any fire emergencies. Not that a town of 500 people would have very many.

Viper and his deputy commander, a massive human being who calls himself Sidewinder, are seated behind a folding table, wearing their usual fatigues. Behind them is an American flag on a pole and a banner that reads **TRUE PATRIOTS: DEFENDING OUR FREEDOM**.

Sean and I grab seats in the back row as an animated conversation about a proposed gun law continues.

An old man in front is on his feet, waving his arms. He's angry and urging everyone to fight.

"First, they force us to wear masks. Now they're coming for our God-given guns!"

"You're right, Harvey," Viper says. "Something has to be done. We can't just stand by and let our constitutional rights get taken from us. Am I right?"

The 17 other people in the audience whistle and cheer.

"That senator better not step foot in this neck of the woods," another man warns. He's wearing oil-stained denim coveralls and sipping black coffee from a Styrofoam cup. "It'll be the last thing she does!"

"Target practice!" someone yells.

Viper clasps his hands together as if he's in church. "Amen, brothers, amen."

He resembles a pricey personal trainer with his perfect teeth and toned physique. The wrinkles around his ice-blue eyes and threads of gray running through his medium beard only add to his allure.

"Well, what are we going to do about that damn bill?" Harvey demands. He's still worked up. Spittle is spraying. "How can we stop it?"

Sidewinder whispers something in Viper's ear, making the commander nod.

"My friend, did you happen to see the video of our little drive-by in Portland the other day?" Viper asks Harvey.

"I sure did. Way to scatter those libs, put the fear of Jesus in them!" Several in the crowd laugh.

Viper shows no emotion. He calmly scans the crowd. His steely gaze locks onto me for an instant, giving me shivers.

"Well, let's just say we're cooking up something big in response to that gun bill in Washington," he says. "And it won't be with paintball guns."

"Tell us more!"

"Folks, you know I can't, at least not in public." He eyes me again. "You never know who's listening."

That seems to satisfy everyone. Heads bob with knowing nods.

The agenda moves on to other topics, all of them fairly ordinary.

There's a reminder that the pro-police "Back the Blue" rally in Salem has been set for March 10 – everyone please put it on your calendar is the message. After that there's a fundraiser at the Kellerman farm and the annual skeet shoot, which also raises money, the crowd is told. The top prize this year is a freezer full of venison, Sidewinder announces, drawing a few ahhs.

We stay until the end. I'm feeling buoyed, thinking Sean couldn't possibly want to join this group and its geriatric membership now.

We're on our feet when Viper comes our way.

"Have we met?" he asks me.

"Not exactly. I'm Robb; this is Sean. We were in Portland on MLK Day."

Viper's expression instantly turns cold. He drinks in our longish hair, my worn Pearl Jam T-shirt.

"Which side were you on?" he asks.

"Neither," I say, suddenly nervous about having wandered into a lion's den. "Came to see you, really."

The look of menace on the commander's face dissolves. "Oh, that's good. For a minute there, I thought Sidewinder would have to take you both out."

Up close the deputy is the biggest man I've ever seen. A walking mountain. His shaved head tops a fire hydrant of a neck. His hands are sledgehammers. He looks indestructible, like a Marvel super-villain.

"What about you?" Viper asks Sean.

"We heard about the truck parade, had to check it out. Awesome, man. Especially the paintball guns."

Viper seems pleased, offering a serpentine grin that slithers through his beard.

"Every time we do an event, we get more members. We shoot our own videos, mainly to protect against the other side's false allegations. But when we post, the reaction is almost always good for us."

I cringe as he calls incitement to riot an "event."

"Well, welcome," he continues. "You're both probably a little young to be ex-military. Are you hunters? We can always use men who can shoot straight."

We shake our heads.

Viper looks disappointed, prompting Sean to blurt, "But we're good at military tactics and stuff like that."

"Oh yeah? How's that?"

"Video games mostly."

Sidewinder cackles. Coming from the behemoth the laughter breaks like thunder, making the chairs tremble.

"Don't mind him, he's easily amused," Viper says as the roar continues. "Thank you both for coming. See you around."

The militia men turn and walk away, shaking hands with the old folks as they go. Before they disappear through a back door, I can hear Sidewinder bellow: "Video games! Hah!"

I look at Sean, whose head is hanging. "That was stupid," he whispers.

"Nah," I say, putting an arm around his shoulders and steering him toward the parking lot. "You do know a lot about tactics, dude. I would have said the same thing."

"Really?"

"You bet. Let's get out of here and smoke some weed."

Privately, I'm elated. Sean was rejected by the very men he'd been idolizing. Maybe going to the meeting wasn't such a bad idea after all.

As we're driving, passing a fat joint back and forth, Sean asks what I thought of the meeting.

"Nearly put me to sleep, dude. We were the youngest people there, by about 40 years."

"And Viper?"

"Pretty intense. Did you see his mood change in a flash like that? Scary."

"Yeah, intense," Sean says. He's got a far-off look in his eyes that troubles me.

"Hey, Burrito Supreme, whatcha thinking?"

Sean faces me and smiles.

"Ever been to a gun range?" he asks.

———

It's a banner day. I sell the used tandem bicycle that had been in my window for a few weeks to a young couple who'd just moved to town.

The newlyweds paid in cash – more than enough to take Layla out to a nice dinner and drinks. I rush back to the River Vista and head up to her apartment.

The door is opened by Mandy, who doesn't recognize me. She's looking stylish with a rust-colored wool scarf over a sleeveless cashmere top and black leather leggings.

"Layla, someone for you."

"We've met before," I say. "I'm Robb."

"Oh, sorry about that. I'm terrible with faces. Or maybe I just need to wear my glasses more."

Layla steps over to give me a hug, but I can see worry on her face. "We're talking about maybe doing an exhibit."

"With as many pieces as you can share," Mandy says with a big smile.

"I'm honored," Layla tells her. "We'll see. I don't know if I'm ready yet."

"Trust me, you are. There's a cosmic flow in your work – chaos, urgency, pure energy. Each of your paintings conjures up powerful emotions."

I nod. In just a few words, she's summed up everything entrancing about Layla's art – except for the sensuality that maybe only I can see.

"I should go," the gallery owner says, glancing at her slim silver watch. "Let's talk more about this later."

After Mandy leaves, her heels tapping Morse Code on the wooden stairs, Layla turns to me.

"Are you here to tell me how the militia meeting went?"

"Over dinner? I scored some cash today and we need to celebrate your first exhibit offer. I'm so proud of you."

"Sorry, sweetie," she says, touching my cheek with her long fingers. "Not tonight. I feel a bit unsettled. Think I'll paint."

I give a good-natured nod, but she reads the disappointment on my face.

"Well, if you don't mind eating late … I do want to hear about Sean and the militia."

"How's 8?" I say, rejuvenated.

"Make it 9."

"Mexican and margaritas?"

"Sushi and sake."

"You got it."

I gallop down the stairs only to be stopped by someone calling my name. It's Aliston, doing his Whac-a-Mole thing.

He steps into the hall with a rare grin on his face. He usually seems so dour, oddly hunched for a slender, 42-year-old man. I remember how he raced through the lobby a few days ago, nearly knocking me down.

"I've hit the big time," he says. "Alex Austin. Can you believe it?"

"Oh, wow," I say, feigning interest, as is often the case with Aliston and his assorted ill-fated business ventures. Something about the name sounded familiar, though.

"The congresswoman?"

"Senator. Her people reached out to me. I'm still on Cloud Nine. They're putting me in charge of promoting her North Coast appearances, starting with a televised town hall, right here at the Liberty. National TV, Robb!"

"Super awesome, man. Fulltime job?"

"Could become one, I think. She's sponsoring that monumental gun control bill. A real game-changer. If that passes, she could run for the White House. And I'd be in on the action."

"Sweet, but what about your other gigs?"

Aliston told me a coupla weeks ago that he was midway through a horror novel about a poisonous cloud driven by an alien force tentatively titled "It Kills from Above" and fine-tuning software for an app that would "revolutionize the way we trade stocks." The app had been on the brink of being released for five years now.

"On hold – even the day trading. Big learning curve. Never did press for a big-time politician before."

"Well, congrats and good luck."

"Thanks, Robb. See you around!"

Aliston returns to his apartment and I catch a glimpse of his ever-expanding computer array. Two large monitors with screens filled with stock charts, and a long steel desk dotted with hard drives, headphones and keyboards. It fills his entire living room. I shake my head thinking what a waste. It's a killer set-up for video games.

I grab Mrs. Wong's mail, plus a couple of her latest boxes from Amazon. I pull out the catalogues, leaving them behind.

She opens her door before I can knock.

"Afternoon, Mrs. Wong," I say, presenting the day's delivery.

She raises the biggest box to her chin for a close look at the shipping label and smiles, creating new Etch A Sketch artwork with the lines in her face.

"Come in, my boy," she says, shuffling off to the kitchen just as her tea kettle begins to whistle.

I follow, fully expecting either a cup of green tea or bowl of soup. Both homemade. It was her way of thanking me for bringing the mail and performing other small favors.

She calms the kettle and waits for me in the middle of the kitchen. Then she points to the cabinet over the fridge. Mrs. Wong stands 4-foot-8, and her sister has forbidden her from using a stepladder after a couple of nasty falls, so whatever she has in there is likely seldom seen.

I open the oak cabinet door and see a few dusty liquor bottles and a red wooden case emblazoned with Chinese lettering in gold leaf. I place my hand on the case like a TV game show model and look down. A snowy head bobs.

"Yes, yes! You open."

I place it on the table, flip the silver latch. Inside is a stack of yellowed letters and a small, black felt box. I show her the box, drawing a toothy smile.

She brushes it clean, then opens the lid, presenting it to me in her creased palms.

I see a gold ring with a large emerald in the middle. Beautiful and radiant. A woman's ring, judging by the size of the band.

"For your girl," Mrs. Wong says, delighted. "You give."

"Layla?"

"Yes, yes! The one for you. Very special."

I look closer at the ring, see the jewel glowing in the afternoon light peeking through the curtains. There are etchings of dragons on each side of the band. Dragons are Layla's favorite, as evidenced by her biggest tattoo, but there's no way Mrs. Wong could have known that.

"I can't accept it," I say. "Besides, she has no interest in being tied down."

"She in love. Even blind woman can see."

"Well, if she's in love with me, she's never said so," I say, surprising myself with how sad the words sounded.

The next thing I know, Mrs. Wong is stuffing the box in the front pocket of my cargo pants.

"No, I can't. It's probably worth a fortune."

What would her sister say if she knew the treasure was being given away – to the dude who takes out the trash? Probably think I conned her somehow. I reach down to get the box, feel bony hands grip my wrist.

"You keep, my dear. If girl say no, you give back."

"Why do you think she loves me?"

Mrs. Wong flashes that knowing smile again. "You not only one who likes my tea," she says.

My ancient upstairs neighbor. Matchmaker and fortune teller.

"The ring – did you buy it?" I look around the apartment, see how jammed it is with recent purchases. There's a shiny new juicer on the counter, next to a bread machine and toaster oven that are still in their cartons. The table is piled high with Amazon pouches that have yet to be opened.

"No, silly boy. For many years I wear, with much joy. But ring not for old woman. It sleeps, waits …" She stabs my chest with a gnarled finger. "For you!"

There's a brief silence while I await the story behind the dragon ring. Her sister told me she'd never married, but had she been engaged? Was it a family heirloom?

But there's no tale. Instead, Mrs. Wong pushes me toward the door.

"I shop now. You give. Lovely girl."

————

The ring is hiding in my dresser behind balled socks as Layla and I enter Tokyo Grill.

The place is usually jammed, but it's near closing time and just two of the booths lining the plate-glass windows are filled.

A certain River Vista octogenarian is on my mind as the first wave of food arrives: a cup of miso and a side spinach salad with honey-ginger dressing.

"I didn't know you and Mrs. Wong were pals," I say, blowing on a spoonful of steaming soup.

"She's a trip," Layla says, smiling. "Her stories are amazing."

"Stories? About what?" *A ring, perhaps?*

"Oh, from her past … in China. Did you know she fought the Japanese when she was 8? Served the commanders poisoned chicken. They all dropped dead. Crazy, huh?"

Luen Wong, World War II heroine. What else had I been missing?

"How did you get that out of her?" I ask, incredulous. "She never tells me anything about her past."

"Do you ever sit down with her? She's a real chatterbox."

"You're kidding."

"Well, I do have an advantage," Layla says, deftly snaring spinach leaves with her chopsticks. "I speak a little Mandarin."

My eyebrows shoot up. Another thing I didn't know about her.

"What? You've never been to China."

"No, but my dad once taught American history there, at the university in Shanghai. I picked it up from him growing up, but my vocabulary is pretty limited."

"Oh my God, your father taught in China? Next you'll tell me your mom was an astronaut."

Layla laughs. "No, just a poet, actress and playwright. But they never did anything for long. Too boring."

I shake my head. My dad is a plumber and my mom stayed home to raise four kids. No mystery there. The sushi rolls arrive and I snag one filled with shrimp and seaweed. I'm usually clumsy with the sticks and tonight is no exception. The food falls into a small bowl of soy sauce, amusing Layla.

Recovering my honor, I toast her artistic success with sake.

"To my favorite painter of all things abstract and mystical, may Bellissima be the start of your next great adventure. Soon, everyone will know how incredibly talented you are."

Layla blushes, a rare sight.

"Thanks Robbie, but you know I don't think I'm ready. A few pieces on the side, sure, but an exhibit all about me?"

It's a funny thing about my relationship with Layla. I'm insecure about us; she's just as insecure about her art – to the point of self-sabotage.

What she creates on canvas is so intensely introspective, a window deep into her soul, that I think revealing it to the world is a frightening prospect. Like walking down the street stark naked. She's faked illnesses before to get out of appointments with people who wanted to show her paintings. There's little I can do, other than keep cheering her on.

I probed a little one time and she told me it might be genetic, this reluctance to share her art.

Her father had written a half-dozen books chronicling his wanderings and never sent them to publishers. The manuscripts just gathered dust in an old green steamer trunk. Her mother had written even more plays, but those weren't in the trunk. They were all in her head, never to be put to paper.

Layla asked her parents once why they didn't let others see their art. Didn't they fear all that work would be lost? Or worse, never be heard or read?

Her mother just laughed and squeezed her tight. "You will pass them on to your children like jewels, and then they to theirs. And so, nothing will be lost."

Layla puts down her chopsticks, manages to push the sudden sadness from her eyes.

"Tell me about your encounter with those militia fools. I'm dying to know how it went."

"Incredibly boring. Bunch of seniors in a room at the firehouse, griping about gun control. Then they talked about an upcoming fundraiser. That's about it."

"Really?"

"Yeah, I kinda thought they'd be firing off guns and whooping it up, like some old Western."

"And Sean?"

"They made fun of him."

"*What?*"

"The leaders came over to us after, and I guess they're looking for new members, because they asked if we had any military training."

"What did Sean say?"

"He said he plays video games and they cracked up. Sean was bummed, but I thought it was a good thing. You know, maybe put an end to his flirtation."

"That *is* a good thing."

"Yeah, but there's more. He now wants me to go with him to the local shooting range. I opened his laptop yesterday and saw he'd been searching how to get a gun permit."

Layla gasps and reaches across the table to squeeze my hand. "Robb, you can't let him do that. He's not like you. If he joins those crazies, he'll do anything they ask."

"I know. I'll think of something." I drop another chunk of sushi and this time Layla's expression doesn't change. She just stares at me with those wood-grain eyes in a rueful way.

"Sorry," she says, breaking her own trance. "Don't mean to be such a downer. I trust you to do the right thing. Just be careful."

"I will," I say. "Now … what did Mrs. Wong say about me?"

CHAPTER
SEVEN
VIPER

THE RATS ARE coming straight at us.

A man, a woman, a young boy. The man's white cotton shirt is plastered against his torso with sweat. His right arm is around the woman's waist, helping her up an embankment of red dirt and creosote bushes.

I adjust the focus on my night vision goggles. The woman looks to be about seven months' pregnant. The boy is maybe 8 years old. He's wearing a softball shirt and a Dodgers cap streaked with mud.

It's been a long, hard journey by the look of them, but they're on American soil now, and they're not invited. They're stinking rats. All of them. And soon, one way or another, they'll be sent back to wherever they came from.

I stroke the barrel of the AR-15 waiting at my side like a faithful dog. I could pick them off, easy as can be, but this is not Iraq. This is not a war zone – at least not yet. This arid place is the last mile of Arizona, the southern border, and these people are illegals, trying to suck off the teat that is our great county. Take our jobs. Change the complexion of America.

I'm kneeling on a bluff, watching the family below. They're slowly approaching, winding their way through scattered mesquite trees and patches of tall, dry grass.

With our military-grade night gear, we can see the green figures coming. They're less than a quarter-mile from our position.

My earpiece comes alive. It's Sidewinder.

"Viper, you seeing this?"

"Roger that," I say. "Take Ratchet and Maverick and flank them. I don't want the rats making a beeline back to the border. They're ours now."

"Copy."

Confident that they can't see me on a moonless night, I get to my feet and secure the assault rifle in my chest sling. I check my handgun, making sure a bullet is in the chamber. *Locked and loaded.*

The rule is not to engage without the express approval of Border Patrol. Observe and report. But there are no federal agents within 30 miles. By the time they get here, the rats will have scurried away. So, to hell with calling the feds.

We're the goddamn enforcers now.

I start making my way down to the family, in no particular rush. Sidewinder reports over the radio that everyone is in position.

"I'll do the meet and greet," I say.

Looking forward to it. Watching the sheer terror on the faces of the Mexicans and Salvadorans when they see our guns and realize they're surrounded is one of my fondest joys. Not quite Christmas morning, but right up there.

The woman spots me first and screams. The man instinctively steps in front to shield her. The boy grabs his mother's left leg.

"Don't shoot!" the father says in English. "Don't shoot!"

He's looking at me with wide eyes, half begging, which is part of the fun. I've got my sidearm pointed at his heart. My entire True Patriots unit – five of my best men – are ringing them in.

No need to watch your six when you're in the Arizona desert, American soil. It's nothing like Fallujah.

I give my men a downward wave and they lower their guns.

"Frisk the man," I say. Sidewinder, all 6-foot-4, 325 pounds of him, steps forward to do the job.

"Just a pocket knife," he says, tossing it to me. It's an old Swiss Army Knife, scratched and dirty.

My Spanish is limited, so I look over at Boomer and give a nod. He's white, but he spent time in Argentina with his family and learned the language.

"Que hacias aqui?" he asks the man. "A donde vas?"

The father removes his filthy straw hat and wipes his brow with a blistered hand. "We come from Honduras," he answers. "A long journey, señor."

"Tell him they've been caught crossing the border," I say to Boomer.

Te ha pillado cruzando la frontera.

Understanding that I'm in charge, the man turns to me with pleading brown eyes. "Por favor, señor, nosotros queremos asilo."

He's seeking asylum.

"Ask him why he thinks he deserves to live in this country," I say.

The trembling man tells Boomer that his family is fleeing warring gangs that have been making life miserable in San Pedro Sula. Many innocent people have died simply because they've been in the wrong place at the wrong time. After an uncle was gunned down by mistake and their son was nearly killed in a crossfire while walking home from school, they decided to leave. It was either flee or die.

America is the only place where they think they can be safe and also have opportunities, he says. Jobs, a home, good schools.

He's Juan, a butcher by trade. His wife, Gabriella, is a teacher. They are honest, hard-working people. They detest the drugs and violence infesting their homeland. They long for a better life.

Boomer translates the familiar story and I feel my blood pressure rising. All these filthy illegals. It's always the same: They come here asking for favors, seeking sympathy, but all they really want is a slice of our hard-earned pie. Our jobs, our way of life. And then what do they do? Bring in their drugs and their gangs. Desecrate our communities.

If it was up to me, I'd shoot them all. Bury them in the desert. That's the only taste of American soil I'm willing to give the rats.

Sidewinder moves to my side.

"Border Patrol?"

"Not yet," I say. "Let's send a message first."

I step forward, stopping less than two feet from the man, who is now perspiring and trembling. The woman begins to beg in Spanish, the boy clinging to her side.

"Por favor, no! Por favor, no!!"

I'm so sick of these parasites. I pistol-whip the man, forcing him to his knees. He should thank me for the important lesson, but instead he clasps his hands in prayer. That ticks me off.

I kick him hard in the gut and he tumbles silently onto the dirt.

"Search them," I command.

The man has nothing left on him but a canteen, but the woman has a bundle of cash in a zippered bag buckled around her swollen belly. These illegals are always carrying dollars it seems. Seed money for their new life. Or just what little is left after paying the coyotes who ferry them across.

There is $500 in twenties and fifties. I pocket it as an "enforcement fee," to be shared equally by my crew.

To Boomer, I say, "Tell him to get up and take his family back where they came from. Tell him we'll be watching."

The man slowly rises to his feet, dusts himself off. Then, saying nothing, he takes his wife's hand and turns to head south. The boy looks at me with hate – the kind of hate I'd seen on the faces of so many Iraqis – before following his parents.

"Viper, you're letting them go?" Sidewinder asks.

"Depends. If he heads straight south, the man lives. If he doesn't ..."

Three of us head back to the bluff, where we lie down with our rifles. There's a pause while sights are adjusted with a few clicks.

The family is moving slowly, shaken by their encounter. The border wall – and the hole they crawled through – is only a few yards away. They could return to Mexico, regroup and try again later.

But there's something in the man's eyes. Defiance or maybe just determination. After a perilous trek, they'd made it to America. A brief but exhilarating taste of freedom.

If the family ran into the Border Patrol, the agency would be duty-bound to hold them and process their request for asylum. True Patriots has no such obligation.

At the hole in the wall, the man and his wife talk. He's pointing west to a dirt trail, she's shaking her head.

I have them in my sights. My finger is on the trigger.

What are you going to do, Juan the Butcher?

He looks all around, then takes his wife's hand and leads her west, trying to get around us.

They're all just stinking rats. We gave them a chance.

"Take him out," I say.

All three guns fire. The bullets hit their mark. Juan is sent flying against the wall.

I instruct Sidewinder to go down and dump the body on the Mexico side, where it can serve as a grim warning to others. Border Patrol can thank us later.

My deputy commander salutes and heads down, his massive frame disappearing into the night.

I hear the woman's wails despite the distance, but I feel no emotion.

We trapped some rats. You can't just set them free.

CHAPTER
EIGHT
ROBB

I'D NEVER BEEN to a shooting range before. Or fired a real gun. Just water pistols and the plastic rifles at the arcade.

As I step inside Rory's Guns & More, I'm a jumble of nerves. Sean is like a kid making his first trip to Disneyland.

I can understand why. Guns & More lives up to its name. There really is more. Much more. The gun store is inside a converted warehouse on the east end of town, facing a gravel parking lot. But keep walking and it opens into a shooter's paradise.

On one side there's a target range with a dozen lanes, and on the other a sprawling combat shooting course with faux building facades and pop-up bad guys.

We'd been told that off-duty cops tested themselves quite often in a friendly competition preceded by frantic wagering. There was also an annual competition that drew marksmen from throughout the Pacific Northwest. Framed pictures of past winners lined the wall behind the cash register.

"There's Viper," Sean says, practically swooning. "Six years ago."

It's a Wednesday afternoon and nobody is using the course, so there's not much action to observe. Sean is too eager to shoot a gun for the first time to mind.

Since we're beginners, we pick .22-caliber pistols. One of the employees, a skinny 21-year-old with bad acne named Larry, goes over the safety rules and gives us basic instructions.

Larry had some kind of deep South drawl that made some of his words hard to understand, so we keep asking him to repeat himself. "Fire" came out sounding like "fay-er." "Aim" was "ay-yum."

Finally, we're ready. Sean and I had already wagered $20 on the best shooting, so I felt the competitive juices flowing. Losing to Sean was never a good idea. He'd rub it in for days and days.

Alone in my lane, I slide on my earmuffs and safety glasses and aim my gun at the paper target of a head and torso suspended 40 feet away. Then I squeeze the trigger. The first few shots stray far from the boundaries of the target, but then I steady myself, account for the recoil and try again.

This time, I do better, actually hitting the target-man's torso. Unfortunately, I was aiming at the head.

A few rounds later, I press the button that sends the target reeling to me on a wire, then pull it down. Not too bad. Some of the errant rounds were closer than I thought, a lazy semi-circle by the right ear and shoulder.

I'm still assessing my debut when I hear Sean celebrating next door.

He comes running over with his target. Smiling broadly, he points to the head, which has been drilled four times. There's another group of holes in the chest.

"I'm a fucking dead-eye!" he exclaims.

Larry appears, shaking his head in astonishment. "Day-am, fella! Butter mah butt and call me a biscuit!"

Rory Bellwether, the portly owner, hustles over to see what the commotion is about. Looking at Sean's target, he nods in approval.

"That's good shooting, son. Excellent clusters."

Glancing at my paper, the owner pats me on the shoulder. "Practice makes perfect. Don't get discouraged."

Bellwether waddles off and I see Sean grinning at me. "Pay up, sucka," he says.

That was the hard-and-fast rule between the two of us. The loser had to pay up immediately. No "I'll get you later" or partial payments. I dig a twenty out of my wallet and he swipes it from my fingers.

He begins spouting off shooting tips, like he's suddenly an expert. It's infuriating, but he's better than me, so I stand there and listen.

We do one more practice session at a longer distance – no bet this time – and I land three body shots. Sean does even better than before, with six head shots and a couple more in the heart.

My plan is quickly becoming a disaster. I'm trying to talk my buddy out of joining True Patriots, but it turns out he's something of a shooting prodigy. My task just got tougher.

In the parking lot, Bellwether stops us, nearly out of breath. He tells Sean about a big shooting competition coming up in a few weeks.

"A lot of cops compete, and there's always some of the TPs," the owner says.

"TPs?" I ask.

"True Patriots. You fellas heard of them?"

"Yeah, sure," Sean says brightly. "We went to their last meeting."

"Is that right? Well, them boys can shoot, take it from me. But so can you. Don't know if I caught your name."

"Sean McNalley."

They shake hands. "You should sign up, young buck. Prove yourself," Bellwether says.

I silently groan. There's no way Sean can resist such a tempting challenge, I know. And I'm quickly proven right.

"I'm in," he tells the gun merchant with a smile. "Sounds like fun."

———

Talisman's house is a glorified shack with an aluminum pipe for a chimney. There are chickens – the free range variety, apparently – scattered through the yard.

The property is accessed by a rutted dirt road that drops suddenly and steeply from the two-lane highway down to mudflats on the outskirts of town.

I walk past his rusting pickup, note the frayed **ISIS HUNTING PERMIT** sticker on the rear bumper. This is his place all right.

The front stairs are rotting. They bend, groaning, under my weight.

With a start, I see curtains move and a disheveled man staring at me. Then the door swings open with a loud creak. I expect to see the barrel of a loaded shotgun, but he merely ushers me inside.

"You must be Robb, the one who called." His hair is wild in an Einsteinian way and his graying beard is long enough to be braided, which it is – in three places. He emits a musky scent like a wild animal. "Come in."

"Thanks."

Before I can sit he presses a shot glass in my hand filled with an amber liquid.

"My own whiskey. Best in town."

He downs his and I do the same. It's God-awful moonshine that burns my throat like gasoline. I suppress the desire to gag.

Recovering, I say, "So, I understand you co-founded True Patriots."

"Yeah, me and Clarence. He goes by Viper."

"Sounds like you two had a falling out."

"You could say that. It never would have worked out, though. He had to be the alpha. There wasn't room for the two of us."

He's in a rocking chair made out of logs and branches. I'm on a tattered couch covered with a wool blanket. A black cat is curled on the floor, enjoying the warmth of a wood stove.

"My buddy has just discovered guns. He's thinking of joining TP," I say. "He thinks it'll be fun."

Talisman's face fills with alarm, animating his bushy eyebrows. He leans forward and grips my hand hard.

"You can't let him do that," he says, lowering his voice. "They'll turn him into something else. He'll never be the same."

"W-what do you mean?

He releases me, leans back and sighs.

"It's not the Boy Scouts. The shit these men are into – it's real, man."

"Like what?"

"What they do on the border. Their attacks on gays and Blacks. Hey, I served with Viper in Iraq, so I know what he's capable of. He did some nasty shit over there as our platoon leader, but we were surrounded then by ragheads. Almost impossible to know which ones were on our side and which would shoot you in the back if given half a chance.

"When I got out, I started True Patriots to keep our oath, defend this country against threats foreign and domestic. Then Viper comes along with a mountain of a chip on his shoulder. Starts preaching about how immigrants and liberals and BLM are coming to take away our rights, and we have to take up arms to defend ourselves.

"Viper turned what I started into something ugly. I wanted to achieve change at the ballot box, man. You know, embrace conservative values, keep the government from crushing people who refuse to conform, like what happened at Ruby Ridge and Waco. But Viper kept talking about uniting the militias, taking out 'treasonous' senators and governors with bullets, not ballots.

"He's crazy and I had to get out, but he has his followers – some in high places. Your friend, if he throws in with them, he's …"

He trails off, gets up to pour himself another shot. Downs it immediately.

"Viper has this fantasy of leading an armed revolt," he continues. "The boogaloo."

Talisman sees the confusion on my face.

"The next civil war," he explains. "Armed insurrection, man, from coast to coast. That what he's after. He calls regular people 'sheep,' says he's the herder. In his mind, everyone who disagrees with him is an FBI plant. Paranoid son of a bitch put a gun in my face once – accused me of being a traitor to the cause. That was a little more than a year ago. Haven't seen him since.

"Like I said, he's the alpha," he says quietly, but with a dose of sadness. "His way or the highway."

"You're describing a dangerous man."

"Yeah, I suppose that's right. I checked his worst impulses, but with me out of the picture Clarence can do whatever he wants to do, say whatever he wants to say."

I shake my head. "Some of things he says online are pretty effed up."

"And that's just what he wants you to see. Tip of the iceberg. He's always cookin' up something, that one."

What Talisman is saying spooks me. *What is Sean getting himself into?* I feel like running out the door and never looking back.

Instead, I rise to my feet and thank the odd, hairy man for his time.

"You've given me a lot to think about," I say. A whopper of an understatement.

I'm nearly at my car when he calls to me from his rickety porch.

"Hey, kid! Tell your friend to watch his six."

CHAPTER
NINE
ROBB

AS IF I WASN'T freaking out enough, I quickly learned that Sean had slipped into full-bore tournament training mode.

He'd stopped playing video games. All of them. He was staying away from bars and had moderated his habit of firing up a bowl of Oregon homegrown after work.

The bulk of his spare time was spent at Rory's or on his laptop doing "research," which mostly consisted of reading True Patriots social media feeds. He'd practically memorized Viper's Twitter rants. The commander's angry slogans had become his own.

Making matters worse, he began listening to far-right podcasts and radio shows. His view of the world, which wasn't terribly large to begin with, was shrinking dramatically.

I finally sat down with him to share what I'd learned about True Patriots and Viper. To his credit, he listened. But when I was finished, he just looked at me and shook his head.

"Do you really believe what the liberal media tells you?" he asked. "It's all bullshit, dude. Wake up."

The new attitude was astonishing, since Sean had never cared about anything even remotely political before. If the subject came up, he'd give me a sleepy look and yawn. I tricked him into registering to vote at the DMV, but to my knowledge he'd never cast a ballot. I guess you can say he preferred to be blissfully uninformed, even about local issues. Whenever I brought a newspaper home, he'd read only the sports section and cartoons.

He went to Portland that night, I suppose, strictly for fun.

So it was shocking to hear words coming out of his mouth like "reclaim America" and "there's no such thing as illegal firearms."

And then one day in late February, things got worse. Much worse.

Sean walked through the door with an aluminum case.

He opened it in front of me, smiling like a proud father with a newborn. Inside was a sleek pistol, a Glock 19 semiautomatic in matte black.

"Whaddya think? It's military grade."

"Sweet, but isn't it expensive? Thought you were saving up for a new game console."

"Nah, not anymore. Besides, Rory gave me a great deal."

I did my best not to show my true feelings as a ripple of uneasiness moved through me.

"Cool," was all I could muster.

"Check it out," he said, holding the weapon in his right hand. "It's 9mm, but light and compact, with a manual safety. Rory says that's a bonus feature for a Glock."

He flipped the small black lever up and down with his thumb.

Sean handed the gun to me like a proud father. It was seductive, filling my hand perfectly as if built to order.

"Feels nice," I said.

"Everybody in the tournament has their own gun. Gonna start

practicing with it tomorrow. You should come. Want to try the course with me?"

"No, but I'll come and watch. Every competitor needs fans, right?"

After that, I had to see Layla. My chat with Talisman had been unnerving. So was seeing Sean's gun. I needed her advice.

We meet at my favorite taproom, the one where Christie works part-time and sometimes slips me a free pint. She's not there, though, which is a bummer. It's a small downtown brewery in a converted used-car showroom. There isn't a river view or anything, so it's seldom crowded. Just what I wanted – a quiet place to talk.

I'm sitting anxiously at an oak barrel table when Layla walks in wearing Ray-Bans, her Dua Lipa hair bouncing off her shoulders, one of which is bare. Several older men turn to watch. I can't blame them.

"What's the matter? You sounded upset," she says, pulling up a stool.

"Let me grab you something first. IPA?"

"That'd be great, thanks."

I return with the beer, clink her glass with my own. I decide to get straight to the point. None of my usual awkward meandering.

"Sean bought a gun. I'm freaking out."

Layla nearly spits out her hoppy brew. "*A gun?* What kind of gun?"

"A Glock," I say. "Choice of cops and criminals alike."

"Dear God."

"It gets worse. He's at the shooting range almost every night now, practicing for a tournament."

"What the fuck?"

"My feelings exactly. He wants to impress Viper by winning the trophy."

"If he does, they'll probably want him to join. What can you do?"

"I tried sitting him down and talking to him. It didn't go well. But maybe you can do better. You're better at persuasion than me. You won the debate prize in school, after all."

"You remember that? How sweet." She strokes the top of my hand. "But you're his buddy. I'm just the girl in the building who's always on him for being a lazy ass."

"Nah, he knows how smart you are. He'd listen to what you say."

"I don't know …" Her expression changes. Then changes again.

"But you have to move fast," I say. "The tournament is in two weeks and some of the militia dudes are competing."

"What if he does really badly? Maybe this whole obsession will disappear."

"That's what I thought at first, but he's really good. The owner calls him a 'natural.'"

"More like a cash cow for his business," Layla says, frowning.

"You got that right. Shooting at the range isn't cheap. The tournament entry fee is a hundred bucks."

"Thanks for letting me know about Sean," she says. "I can see how worried you are. I'm worried, too. If he gets sucked down that rabbit hole, he won't be the same."

That's what Talisman said.

"Yeah, it's right up there with you joining the circus. Please don't."

She snorts. "*Circus?* Robb, you doofus. How do you come up with these things?"

"They just sort of spill out."

"Obviously. Okay, you've convinced me. I'll talk to Sean."

"What are you gonna say?"

"Dunno, but let's do it at the range. I want to check it out."

"Is that a good idea, Lay? It's noisy as hell. The testosterone is off the charts. You'll hate it there."

"For sure," she says, wiping beer foam off her lips. "But I like to know what I'm up against."

———

In just a few weeks, Sean had become a sensation at Rory's. When word spread of his prowess, challengers began lining up. Bets were placed.

He always seemed to win.

When he tackled the combat range for the first time, he missed only twice. I was stunned. Bellwether slapped him on the back, calling it a "rookie record." Strangers seated in the small rack of bleachers applauded.

Then an enormous man came up to him. It was Sidewinder, the militia leader who'd ridiculed him at the firehouse.

"Brother, I had you all wrong," he said. "I pegged you for some kind of nerd or stoner, but you're the best shooter I've ever seen who ain't never served. Sorry if I hurt your feelings the other day."

"No worries," Sean replied, relief filling his face. "See you around."

"You know where to find us, young blood."

Sean had found his sweet spot. A place where he was considered cool – a young man who could handle a gun with skill beyond his years.

When Layla and I show up one night, Sean is surrounded by men congratulating him, as if he'd hit a walk-off homer in the bottom of the ninth.

He sees me and excuses himself.

"Dude!" he says. "I just beat the defending champ. A friggin'

Green Beret."

"Really? That's awesome," I say, trying to smile.

"The tournament is in a few days. I'm ready, man. Hi Layla."

"What do you get if you win?" she asks coolly. "Your picture on the cover of Guns & Ammo?"

"That would be sweet. The top prize is $500, but you also get a trophy. And your name on that plaque over there."

I can tell Layla is far from impressed, but she manages to say with a straight face, "Quite the honor."

"You guys are coming to the tournament, right? It would mean a lot," Sean says, and I'm moved because he's being sincere.

"I wouldn't miss it, buddy," I say.

"Sean, can I talk to you for a minute?" Layla asks. She grabs a bleacher seat and he follows, curious. I stand anxiously nearby, trying not to intrude.

"What's all this about?" she begins. "I mean are you doing this for fun or what?"

"Absolutely. Shooting is a blast, you should try it."

She lets the unintended pun slide. "I guess if you keep it in here, it's not so bad. Out there, though … well, it's like a plague, isn't it? All that violence. All that blood being spilled."

"Wow, Layla. When did you become such a buzzkill?"

I hear that and begin nervously shifting my weight back and forth.

"I'm sorry, Sean. I guess I'm worried that you may be doing this so you can look good in the eyes of those militia guys."

"So what if I am?" Sean says, getting defensive. "They're not so bad, I've checked them out."

"You know that Viper's patrols on the southern border are under investigation?"

"Illegals, taking our jobs," Sean says with disgust. "He's trying to stop an invasion, protect our country."

"Protect us from what? Farm workers and fry cooks?"

Sean shoots me a look that says, *Tell her to shut up*. I shrug and shove my hands in my pockets.

After a frosty silence, Layla asks, "What do you like so much about True Patriots? Maybe you can explain it to me."

"I don't have to explain shit. Why don't you keep your opinions to yourself?"

"Listen to me, Sean. These people you admire, they're ruthless. They hurt people. Viper was dishonorably discharged. He's not someone to put on a pedestal. He's someone to steer clear of."

"Jesus Christ, I thought you came here as a friend. But you want to tear me down, just as I'm about to do something really special. Stay away from me, Layla."

Sean storms off. Moments later, his adoring fans are ringing him again.

I turn to see a tear sliding down Layla's cheek.

"I'm sorry. I think I made things worse."

It's strange to see her so vulnerable. I wipe away her tear, put an arm around her shoulders.

"Hey, I can't get him to think straight either. Appreciate you trying."

"Swing and a miss."

I give her a weak smile. "Is it wrong that I really want him to do badly in the tournament?"

"I want him to finish last," she whispers. "Maybe that will end this nightmare."

CHAPTER
TEN
VIPER

OLD RORY IS on the phone, going on and on about a 25-year-old shooter who set a course record.

"Best I've ever seen at his age," he tells me.

Bellwether is 75 and very little gets him excited these days. He's usually just an old sourpuss, but I take his calls because he's a vet who fought as a young man in the jungles of Vietnam, has an encyclopedic knowledge of guns and ammo, and isn't afraid to take on the radical libs in Oregon.

He's always firing off angry letters to the editor. Like one a day. Some of them even get published – with the swear words taken out. I admire that kind of tenacity.

Besides, he does a fine job of scouting talent for me.

Bellwether describes the shooter and I figure it's one of the friends who came to my meeting. The video gamer.

"Is his name Sean?" I ask.

"Yeah, that's right. Do you know him?"

"Met him the other day. He and his friend. I think they want to join, but they have no military or police experience. They've never even bagged a deer."

"Well, you should come down for the competition. If I was a betting man, I'd put my cash on the kid to win it all."

"Really? Two of my boys are vying for your ugly trophy. They're pretty good. Not as good as me, but pretty good."

"You'll always have my respect as a former champ," Bellwether says. "But this kid … it's unreal. He never misses. Just bought his first gun, too."

"Okay, okay, I'll come down. You've got me intrigued. What about his friend?"

"Pretty mediocre with a gun. Smart, though."

"Anything odd about those boys?"

"What do you mean?"

"Can I trust them?"

"They're just young bucks," Bellwether says. "Not exactly informant material."

"Just the same, keep an eye out. I can't be too careful. Something big is in the works."

"Will do. See you soon."

I hang up and scratch my beard. Sidewinder is cleaning one of his guns at my kitchen table.

"We may have found our disposable assets," I tell him.

We'd been looking for a couple of eager recruits we could put on a high-risk mission and disavow as rogue wannabes if anything went sideways.

The Alex Austin operation seemed the perfect choice. Pair a shooter with a smart dude. Provide just enough intelligence to light the fuse, then turn them loose.

We would have preferred to do the job ourselves, but every time she visited the state, she had a security detail around her like a forcefield. Usually two former cops, heavily armed with bulletproof vests under their clothes. Getting through them to her would require a willingness to incur casualties and trigger a possible shootout with potential collateral damage.

All my work building up True Patriots as a defender of democracy, all my alliances with county sheriffs, would be ruined by that kind of negative exposure.

No, the senator had to be dealt with quietly. Under the noses of her guards. Thanks to our tipsters, we had the perfect place and time. And now, maybe the perfect pair to carry it out.

"They'll be at the competition at Old Rory's," I say. "The two who went to our last meeting. The ones in the back."

"The one named Sean can shoot. I saw it first-hand," Sidewinder says.

"Bellwether claims the kid is the best natural shooter he's ever seen. And, the other one, he's clever. I can tell he's processing everything."

"Sarge, there's no way those newbs can get this mission done without getting themselves arrested or killed." "You're probably right. But I'd rather spare them than any of my best men. Consider it an initiation rite."

"Are you really serious?"

"Let's see how the kid shoots under pressure," Viper says. "Then we'll know."

———

Sometimes, after waking up in the morning, I walk down the stairs and stop to look at the wooden box hanging on the wall.

Sometimes the box looks back.

Sometimes it whispers.

After all I've been through, all the hell I've witnessed, that doesn't seem strange at all – my silent conversations with the box.

Under its glass is a color photo of my Marine squad in the harsh Iraq sun, with me taking a knee on the right. Pinned around the photo are my service medals. Kathleen found them in the attic, buried in my old duffel with my uniform, and insisted that they come out of hiding. She had the uniform pressed, hung it in our closet.

Now, every day, I walk past the artifacts, trying to resist their power.

Kathleen was proud of my service until the dark moods overwhelmed me. I took my fear and anger out on her, became a raging drunk too many times to count. I regret that now, but it's too late.

She couldn't understand why I wanted to bury the past, why I resisted having another portal in the house that could tap into my scarred brain. The box. The shrine to Sgt. Branch – the man I used to be.

My wife encouraged me to join the VFW, where I could deal with my issues with bro hugs and cheap beer. When that didn't work, she supported my efforts to join Talisman in forming True Patriots.

Talisman was a former senior member of my squad and almost as screwed up as me. Serious PTSD from seeing so much death. I took the killing to another level, getting drummed out of the service on suspicion of intentionally killing civilians – even though they deserved it.

I'd watched too many friends in uniform get blown to pieces by roadside IEDs. There had to be payback. So, I strapped ragheads to my own bombs. Had their families watch as I clicked the detonator.

Nobody in my unit said a word. They all understood. But when the brass heard the rumors, they sent me home for "bad conduct." Told me I was lucky not to go to prison for murder.

One night, a few years later, Talisman found me drowning myself in tequila at a seedy east Portland bar and figured TP would give me a new purpose.

Together, we turned it from a self-help group to a militia supporting conservative values. We spoke out against open borders, efforts to teach white guilt in our schools and acceptance of queer and transgender people in our communities. Kathleen had left by then, which was unfortunate since the job of being a commander led me to control my anger and drinking.

The militia lacked focus until a declared enemy of the people was elected to the U.S. Senate. A lib who ran on a pledge to champion extreme gun control. Our membership doubled when Alexandra Austin took office. Every time she spoke out on gun violence, I could count on more recruits. Pretty soon, we had nearly 200 members. Former and current cops, veterans, hunters, ranchers – they despised her as much as I did.

A handful of Oregon sheriffs did, too. They endorsed our agenda and contributed to our operating fund by hiring us as backup crowd control at big events. Privately, they loved our border patrols and drive-throughs, targeting Black activists and antifa. Publicly, they refused to comment when things got a little out of hand. It turned into an excellent relationship.

The idea of punishing Austin wasn't mine. It came from a leader of a national group called Patriot Brotherhood in a secure call.

"You should teach that former teacher a lesson," he said.

"What do you mean?" I asked.

"Make her stand trial. Shut that bitch the fuck up."

"On what charges?"

"Treason, of course," he said. "Crimes against the Constitution cannot go unpunished."

"I wish I could, brother. Believe me."

"You can. You have an army of patriots. No one can stop you. We saw what you did during that Pride event in Salem."

We crashed that party, marching in a tight formation through the heart of it. We left some of them lying on the pavement, dazed and bloodied. A good day.

The Brotherhood leader wanted me to fold TP into their organization, become a Pacific Northwest chapter, but I politely declined the offer. I've never been the sort to take orders from anyone. Even in the military, I did things my way, with maximum force.

But he did get me thinking. About Austin.

A plan began to form. My CIA friend started gathering intel.

Then Sean and Robb came to the firehouse.

CHAPTER
ELEVEN
ROBB

THE COMBAT SHOOTING range at Guns & More is pretty incredible, I must admit.

Judges and fans sit in a covered area that overlooks the course, which is open to the elements and snakes through a pretend city – or at least a couple blocks of one. Gravel berms are set up on three sides to catch stray slugs.

Shooters face an impressive array of stationary and moving targets. Some of the bad guys roll by at a good clip, while others spring up suddenly in doorways and windows.

Sprinkled in are a dozen or so pop-up "civilians" who cannot be shot without suffering a major points deduction. The course requires shooters to reload on the move and finish in less than three minutes.

I have to give Bellwether credit. His combat zone resembles a low-budget Hollywood back lot, with two-story building facades and cars, all made of plywood and painted to be somewhat realistic.

The highest score recorded in the 15 years of competition was 630 points, by a police detective from Portland named Lars Albright. He ended his epic performance in 2015 one kill shot away from a perfect 650.

Sean's most recent practice run through the course raised eyebrows because he managed kill shots on every target. Unfortunately, he also killed a woman carrying groceries – a 25-point deduction.

I knew all this because my friend couldn't stop talking about how close he'd come to perfection. As we drove to the gun range in Sean's pickup, he seemed unusually tense. Not the laid-back dude I'd come to love. I missed that version of him.

"Worried about the course?" I ask to break the silence.

"Nah, I was thinking about Layla. What she said. I know she's rooting against me."

"Not really. She's not like that."

"Then how come she's not here?"

"She has this thing about guns. And she'd rather not hang around the TPs."

"Whatever. You're here. Thanks, pal."

"F'sho. Break a leg," I say as we pull into the parking lot. "I'll be in the stands watching."

I give him a high five and make my way to the bleachers, surprised that they're nearly filled. Maybe a hundred people. I grab a spot on the top of the four rungs as the public address system comes alive with a loud squeal.

"Welcome to the Northern Oregon Combat Shooting Competition," a man with a smooth voice says. "This year's field has set a record with 95 competitors vying for the trophy."

A busty blonde with red lipstick walks past the crowd, smiling and holding the trophy aloft. Layla would have had a field day.

"Thank you, Cindy," the announcer says. "And, of course, none of this would be possible without Rory. Come on out, sir."

Bellwether, who'd been working the cash register feverishly, steps out from behind the counter and does an awkward bow that draws scattered applause.

The announcer then reviews the rules of the competition and introduces the first shooter, a cross between Schwarzenegger and Van Damme, with a powerful physique and a crewcut. His pistol is in a leather holster buckled across his chest. He's wearing knee pads.

A bell rings and the man pulls his gun, which from my vantage point looks huge. Can Bellwether's targets withstand the punishment that's about to be dealt?

The three minutes pass quickly. He does very well, as far as I can tell.

The two male judges at a table on the sideline huddle, then hand a slip of paper to the announcer.

"Well, ladies and gentlemen, we're off to a great start. The score is 595."

I look at the score card that is projected onto a screen for the audience. Crewcut man apparently hit a civilian and missed two targets.

A murmur runs through the crowd. I see Viper, Sidewinder and two other men in fatigues and battle gear are heading over, Bellwether practically glued to their sides.

The bleachers are packed now but somehow the crowd parts enough for the TPs to sit in the center of the first row. I can't tell whether it's a sign of respect or fear.

It takes nearly an hour to get to Sean, but when his name is called I see Sidewinder and Viper watching intently.

The bell sounds and Sean, wearing a side holster, springs into action.

Wielding his new gun, he takes aim at the first bad guy and squeezes the trigger. Perfect.

Two more pops, two more kills. A woman pushing a stroller appears and he swings to his left but doesn't fire. My jaw drops. I'm amazed at how well he's doing on such a challenging course.

Pop, pop, hold, pop, pop, reload. Pop, pop, pop.

He finishes 10 seconds ahead of the final bell, which the people around me find astonishing. As far as I can tell he's aced it, but I won't know for sure until his score card is on the screen.

The wait is agonizing. I can see the judges huddling, disagreeing over something. I'm torn. It's best for Sean to fail, but part of me still wants him to win.

The suspense finally ends.

"Sorry that took so long, folks," the announcer says. "The shooter did not holster his weapon before leaving the course, which is a 5-point safety violation. Otherwise we would have had our first perfect score."

Loud groans pour from the crowd. Viper is shaking his head.

The score card appears in front of us, prompting another wave of protest. Sean hit every target he should and avoided all he shouldn't.

His score is 645. *Amazing.*

There's still a dozen or so shooters to go, but a knot of men are surrounding Sean on the edge of the course, smiling and slapping him on the back. I catch Sean glancing at me with his crooked smile – half thrilled, half embarrassed by all the fuss.

Viper makes his way up the bleachers toward me. He doesn't have to step around the spectators. They magically move enough to give him a straight path.

"Your friend is quite the marksman," he says. "Very impressive."

I give a half nod, not knowing what to say.

"And you? Why didn't you sign up?"

"I've always hated tests," I say, which is the truth.

I hear Viper's laugh for the first time. It's gritty – the sound of a chainsaw ripping through wood.

"Fuck school, right?" he says. "No more rule books, no more teachers' dirty looks."

I think he's trying to quote Alice Cooper but I'm not certain, so I just give another nod.

"Well, tell your pal we came to see him and he's welcome to join – and you, too – if you're still interested. I can brief you more about TP's mission in private. Too many ears around here."

"I'll tell him, thanks."

If the militia puts its claws into him, flatter him, I doubt he could say no. For maybe the first time in his life, he's enjoying standing out, becoming someone worthy of admiration. Now, on the verge of capturing the shooting trophy, his wish is coming true.

The competition is winding down and Sean is still in the lead. I step outside for a bit of fresh air and call Layla, craving a bit more advice.

"He's in first place," I tell her. "Looks like he's going to win the trophy with a near-perfect score. Most points ever."

"Damn."

"It gets worse. Viper and his goons were here. They told me he's in – we both are – if we want to join."

There's a brief silence as Layla absorbs the news.

"I've been thinking about what you said before – about joining to keep an eye on Sean, keep him out of trouble. Out of jail. I think you have to do it."

It's shocking to hear her say it, but it makes sense. I'll be Sean's life preserver, the only one who can penetrate the cult-like bullshit of the militia.

"Lay, I think they're plotting something. It makes me really nervous."

"What do you know?"

"Nothing. Just a feeling. Like how they never talk about anything serious in public. I think they're planning some sort of attack and they need a shooter like Sean. I sat down with that former member and he was really spooky."

"Please talk to Sean again." There is worry in her voice and I love her for it. "Before it's too late."

"Yeah, I will. Thanks for listening."

When I step back inside, the contest is over. Sean is smiling, holding the trophy.

I break through a throng of well-wishers and give him a man hug.

"You did it, buddy," I say. "Way to go."

"It was a nail-biter at the end. Three dudes came within five points of me."

"Yeah, but that deduction of yours was crap. You should've had a perfect score."

"I just wanted to win, that's all," he says.

"Let's get out of here. Beer's on me."

"Sweet," Sean says, raising the trophy again. It's big and gaudy, featuring a man taking aim with a pistol on a stars-and-stripes pedestal supported by an eagle with outstretched wings. "Best day of my life."

My skin crawls because I know it's true.

———

In the pit of my stomach there's a sour feeling, like a flu bug about to burst and exert its sadistic control.

But maybe I've been demonizing True Patriots too much lately. Maybe Talisman is a drama queen with an axe to grind.

I'm thinking this as Sean and I are driving to Viper's farmhouse out in the boonies. The only trace of mankind in this part of the state is the long-neglected road. There are no houses, no fences, no cattle. I wonder how long it'd take for a tow truck to get here if a car fell into a ditch.

"He likes his privacy, I guess," I say as Sean swerves to avoid another pothole.

I grunt and shake my head. "Don't know why we couldn't do this at the firehouse."

I know the reason, though. Viper's paranoid and always thinks he's being spied on. At his remote property, he can control who sees and hears what.

Before I can give an answer or change the subject, Sean straightens in the driver's seat and grins. "There it is!"

I follow the direction Sean's pointing and, true enough, see the gray outline of a home with a large barn off to the side, painted a traditional red. It's set off the road and there are still no fences or markers – only a sign that declares **TRESPASSERS WILL BE SHOT.**

I always thought such signs were bluffs, but with Viper I have my doubts. As we turn onto his driveway I imagine he's watching with a high-powered rifle. Or maybe his hand is resting on a plunger linked to dynamite.

My worries end as soon as we come to a stop about 20 feet from the house. The front door is open and Viper is standing there, leaning casually against the door frame. He's wearing a beige cowboy hat and blue neckerchief, with faded jeans and boots. He looks like a Western movie star with his chiseled features and piercing eyes.

"Morning, boys. Coffee?"

Sean, who downed two Red Bulls on the drive over, shakes his head. I actually wouldn't mind a cup, but I don't want any freebies from a man named after a lethal snake.

I regret my decision as he takes us inside and into the kitchen, where the aroma of fresh-roasted coffee fills my nostrils. We all sit around an oak table that features an impressive lacquered slab that shows off the grain. Probably made it himself.

"Nice place," I say, trying to be polite. I look around and immediately determine that he lives alone.

There are oak floors throughout and high ceilings with thick logs for beams. In the living room, there's a brown leather couch facing a fireplace framed in river rock and a mantle that was once a tree. Various animal heads hang from the walls, including a mountain lion and an elk with impressive antlers.

"My father's old place. He handed the ranch down to me, but I'm no rancher. Don't have the patience for it. Moved here after my wife left. Made some improvements, which you boys will see in a bit. Sure you don't want any coffee?"

I shake my head but find myself licking my lips as Viper tops off his mug. It bears the words Semper Fi, the Marine oath of loyalty.

"What did you do before the war?" I ask.

"I was in college in Eugene with plans to be a structural engineer. But my father became ill and I began working here, helping him out. After he died, I sold off the cattle and enlisted. I wanted to do something meaningful, I guess. Met my wife between tours."

His candor surprises me. I didn't think he'd be so revealing about his past. For a few moments, his guard is down and he seems vulnerable. Then he dives into business.

"Sorry to drag you out here from the city," he says, "but I can't talk plainly in public. And I don't accept any new members without talking to them face to face first."

"Cool," Sean says.

"That's what we figured," I add.

Viper stares at Sean intently, like a gem being appraised. "Congrats on the trophy. I won mine a while back, but your score … well, you should be proud.

"True Patriots is always looking for people who can handle a gun, but who also share common values. We love our country, would gladly give our lives to defend it. When we see politicians and others seeking to erode our constitutional rights, we take action to oppose them. 'Every citizen should be a soldier. This was the case with the Greeks and the Romans, and must be that of every free state.' Thomas Jefferson said that. Does that make sense? Is that something you believe?"

Sean nods eagerly. I reluctantly follow suit.

"Being a member of True Patriots requires courage and strength of character," the commander says. "This isn't a game to us. We pledge to defend the state from terrorism and invasion, but it's more than that. We also do search and rescue and disaster relief as needed, and serve the community with emergency preparedness and education. We're a civilian volunteer organization."

Like the Rotary Club, only with AR-15s.

"What kind of educating do you do?" I ask, trying not to sound cynical.

"Gun safety, survival skills, that sort of thing," Viper says. "We have two battalions, with brigades in more than a dozen communities. We try to be hyper-local and accessible, a visible resource."

"How do your drive-bys and marches in major cities fit in? Seems like you're shaking things up."

Viper nods. For the first time he looks more friendly than formidable.

"And we are. There are times when we have to send a firm message."

He points to the yellow flag pinned to his dining room wall. The one with the coiled rattlesnake ready to strike and the words "Don't Tread on Me" below.

"That flag was flown during the American Revolution, when there were 13 colonies fighting against British coercion and tyranny," he says proudly of the cheap reproduction. "We're facing a different kind of tyranny now, but the threat is the same. We aim to protect America from those who would weaken it – erode our Christian nationalist heritage, shame us for leading this country to greatness. White guilt? Slavery reparations? It's all nonsense, but at the same time we can't allow it to take root. We have to act. We are the defenders of our way of life – a crucial part of the Great Awakening. Not just us, but every militia across the nation."

Viper's eyes are blazing and it's clear he believes what he's spewing, like a wayward evangelical who preaches a brand of hate and intolerance disguised as love and God's will.

"You two are city folk, but if you lived out here in ranch country, you'd understand where we're coming from a little better. You see, in Oregon, the federal government owns some 30 million acres – that's more than half the state. But they're not satisfied. They want to also control private property and industry with environmental regulations and restrictions, choking off our resources. They're putting ranchers, farmers and small businesses into poverty. That's why they revolted at the Malheur refuge and Sugar Pine Mine. And why we stood with them.

"But there is more we can do. Much more. We're expanding our ranks, looking for young, earnest people such as yourselves. So we can move closer to achieving true justice at last. Take bold action."

I want to ask what he's got up his sleeve, but I don't have to. Sean does it for me.

"What action?" he asks.

Viper leans back and exhales. He appears to be debating whether to say anything more. After a few moments, his expression hardens.

"Have you heard of the abomination known as the Mass Shooting Prevention Act?" he asks, spitting out the last words as if they were poison.

"The gun bill," I say, remembering my chat with Aliston.

"That's right. Sponsored by Oregon's own abomination – Alexandra Austin."

Viper's fingers squeeze the table edge. "We're going to give her an education," he says.

I feel a bad case of nerves coming on, crushing my body like a tsunami. What's this man up to?

"But enough of that for now," Viper says, snapping back into his gentleman rancher persona. The change is whip-fast and startling, like his mood swing at the firehouse. Even his voice changes, from ominous to placid. "Let me take you two into the command center. The boys are excited to meet you."

By command center, he apparently means the barn, because that's where he leads us.

The massive wood doors are open and we step through, our eyes adjusting from the bright sunshine.

The first thing I notice is that there are no horses or farm animals. Viper has set up what appears to be an indoor paramilitary training facility. The entire 30-foot-long rear wall is covered with pegboards and hooks, from which are neatly hung an impressive array of weaponry, from assault rifles to what appears to be a portable rocket launcher. There are ammo boxes stacked high, tactical gear in various shades of camo suitable for all geographic regions and seasons, sophisticated communication devices and night vision goggles.

The arsenal had to be worth a small fortune, and likely illegal to some degree, but I resist the temptation to ask questions for fear of being exposed as the newbie I am.

At a large round table, a fair approximation of what King Arthur and his knights might have gathered around, are seated a handful of stout, resolute men who stare at Sean and me as we draw closer.

There are rifles and handguns on the table inches from their beefy hands and I suddenly fear that they will begin shooting at us, possibly as part of some bizarre initiation ritual. *Dance, suckers! Dance!*

They clap instead.

"Here he is. The champ," Sidewinder says, looking at Sean. He rises from the table like a grizzly. The others follow suit.

Viper passes out Rainier beer. There's a series of pops. Our very own eight-can salute.

"To our new members," Viper says. "Welcome, brothers."

"Welcome!!"

"It's a tradition here for the deputy commander to give you your new names," Viper says, glancing at Sidewinder, who nods. "We never use real names here. True Patriots has enemies, so we protect each other's identities as much as possible."

"You'll be Hawkeye," Sidewinder says to Sean, an apparent reference to his sharpshooting skills. Or maybe the dude just likes "The Last of the Mohicans" as much as I do.

Turning to me the giant blurts one word: "Echo."

Hawkeye and Echo. Okey-doke.

Sean turns my way and I expect his usual wry half-smile, like he's aware how ridiculous this is. But that's not the look he gives me.

He's beaming with pride.

Blood drains from my face as the new reality dawns on me.

We're True Patriots now.

CHAPTER
TWELVE
VIPER

THE BOYS RESERVED a small brewery in Portland's Pearl District for the occasion.

When I arrive, the place is packed with True Patriots and their families, plus some of our biggest supporters and donors. I honestly didn't realize we were here to celebrate a birthday – my fiftieth – until I walk through the doors and they burst into applause.

I'm in jeans and flannel, not camo gear. In this city, if you seem like a militia man you get a lot of dirty looks. Sometimes one of the radical libs will spit in your face on the sidewalk, trying to provoke a fight.

That's not a bad thing, really. We often venture into downtown just to stir up shit, cause a street brawl or two. Keeps us focused. An urban tactics training exercise.

But not tonight.

Tonight, there's a cake with candles. Pizza and beer. A bunch of people getting together for a few laughs.

I'm in a good mood when I see him, sipping a dark beer alone by the towering, stainless steel fermentation tanks. With his shaggy mop of blond hair, scruffy whiskers, baggy red Atari T-shirt and dirty Converse sneakers, he doesn't resemble a paramilitary assassin.

"Hey, Hawkeye," I say, walking over. "Glad you could make it."

"Happy birthday, sir."

"You can knock off the 'sir' stuff. That's strictly for missions. Having a good time?"

"Yeah," he says, lifting his pint glass. "Awesome oatmeal stout."

I catch a whiff of pot coming off him, which doesn't surprise me. It'll take some molding, but he'll become one of us. Disciplined and dependable. I have a feeling.

"You see, we're not always so serious," I say, waving a hand at the crowd. Kids are chasing each other. A collie is sniffing a golden retriever. Sidewinder is chuckling with some of the men, causing a minor earthquake.

"If I knew it was your birthday, I would have brought you something," he says, a bit embarrassed.

I give him a sour look. "Ugh, no thanks. But come over here, I have a present for *you*."

Hawkeye follows me over to a corner of the bar. There's a big cardboard box on top. I reach in, and grab a desert camo uniform shirt.

"It's yours. You earned it," I say, handing it to my new recruit. "Looks like it'll fit."

His eyes grow wide and his mouth gapes.

"Seriously? Awesome!"

I reach in the box again, grab a yellow-and-red patch. Our rattlesnake logo.

"Your very own shoulder patch. Now you're official. One of the few and the proud."

He slaps it on the uniform's Velcro square and gives me a high five.

"Thanks so much! Can't wait to show Robb – I mean, Echo."

"Tell your buddy I have one for him, too. Where is he by the way?"

"Out with his girl."

"Ah, so you two aren't attached at the hip," I say, smiling. "Good to know."

"We've known each other forever. Since elementary school."

"That's a good thing, something to treasure. My best friend didn't make it home from Iraq. Shredded by an IED. Still haven't really gotten over it."

Hawkeye looks a little surprised by my candor. He's Gen Z. Probably never talked to a combat veteran before. We all have our deep-seated angst. He'll find that out soon enough.

"Ready to start training?" I ask, changing the subject. "Obviously, you can shoot. Now you need to learn real tactics. Could save your life one day."

"Absolutely, man," he says. "Sign me up."

"Come on out to my place next weekend. You can stay at the house."

"Awesome."

"We'll start with basic assault weapon training and go from there. It'll be you and a few newer members. Sound good?"

"Can't wait."

"Love the eagerness, Hawkeye."

The molding has begun.

I grab him another stout, point at his T-shirt.

"My uncle had one of those consoles back in the '80s," I say. "Centipede, Asteroids …"

"Yeah, the 2600 – fun toy for Boomers." He looks over at Sidewinder, hoping the big man doesn't hear him talking about video games again. "Retro cool now."

"I saw one in an antique store recently," I say with a laugh. "But seriously, I'm considering adding combat sims to our training. Do you think video games could be useful?"

He looks over at my deputy again. Lowers his voice.

"Well, yeah. When you play COD you have to think fast, adapt to new situations. When Robb and I play as partners, you have to watch out for each other, too. Communication is key."

"That's true in real combat as well."

"They try to make it as realistic as possible, but there's no substitute for the real thing, right?"

"Afraid so. If you take a head shot on the battlefield, you don't regenerate. There are no extra lives."

He gives me a curious look.

"What's it like, you know, shooting bad guys for real?"

I look in his eyes and feel a bit jealous. There's only youthful exuberance. No trace of the sorrow I see reflected in the mirror every single day.

"It's fun," I say. "Until they start shooting back."

CHAPTER
THIRTEEN
ROBB

EVERYTHING BEGAN spiraling out of control a few weeks after our induction into True Patriots.

Viper summoned us to a meeting – in the middle of a damp meadow ringed by pines about 20 miles east of Astoria. He's standing there alone when Sean and me arrive.

"Hawkeye, Echo," he says when we reach him, creating a trail of flattened rye grass. He doesn't have to explain the strange location, the fear of being overheard.

Sean is loving this: The intrigue. The secret meeting. The code names.

As for me, my heart's in my throat, beating like a drum. *This can't be good.*

Viper, clad in his camo casual, is stone-faced. He stares us both down for several tense minutes before speaking.

"Unbutton your shirts."

We do as he says and after a minute or so of searching for anything resembling a wire, he seems satisfied.

"I have a mission for you. I need you to strike a blow for freedom.

For America."

My palms start to sweat. I figure he's going to ask us to join a border patrol or crash another gay pride event.

Sean responds with his favorite word: "Awesome."

"Fair warning: This mission is dangerous," the commander says. "You'd be putting your lives at risk, and I want to give you the opportunity to opt out."

"Thank you," I say weakly.

Viper pulls a photo out of his vest pocket and shows it to us. It's the senator he loathes.

"This is the target, Alexandra Austin. She'll be in Astoria in a week to give a speech and hold a press conference. Afterward, she's planning to visit a female friend. We know the time and place. We also know her bodyguards will be kept at a distance."

"How do you—?" I begin, but Viper silences me with an outstretched hand.

"The less you know, the better," he tells me. "We've been collecting intel for some time, tracking her movements. We know it's reliable."

"What's the mission?" Sean asks, unable to contain his excitement.

"We need you to take her. We have a van that isn't traceable that you will use."

Kidnap a U.S. senator? Pure insanity and yet give Viper credit. He makes it sound easy. Like walking a dog.

"And the friend?" I ask, looking for flaws that could sideline this ridiculous plot.

"We'll take care of that. Weasel has a talent for knock-out drugs. She won't be in the condo when you get there. Just wear masks and gloves, and grab Austin when she arrives."

Sean nods, making mental notes.

Viper hands me a burner cell phone. "When you have the target, call me on this. I'll have someone pick her up, bring her to me at a secure location."

He gives Sean a slip of paper that has a date, time and address printed on it.

"That's the condo and when you can expect the senator to arrive," Viper says. "Memorize and destroy it. You'll need to do some recon. There's an alley in back that is partially hidden. Park the van there, and you should be able to get the target out quietly."

This is nuts.

"What are you going to do to her?" I ask.

"Put her on trial. That's all you need to know," he says. "For your protection."

He looks at both of us, one by one.

"So that's the mission. Are you in or out?"

"In," Sean says without hesitation. "Thank you, sir."

I knew at that moment that Sean would do anything for Viper, to prove himself worthy. And I had to do everything I could to protect him.

Surely this scheme will fall apart.

I follow with the slightest of nods.

"Thank you, Patriots."

I can't resist asking one last question, here, in the middle of a meadow.

"This mission, it seems so … drastic. The gun bill is such a long shot. Why not just let it fail like all the rest?"

Viper's face flushes. He balls his hands into fists and for a moment I think he's going to take a swing at me.

"We can't take that chance," he says. "Every day, with every speech, her support grows. She must be stopped now – before it's too late."

———

An anxious silence fills the cabin of Sean's Silverado as we drive home.

I have to find a way to pry him from the militia, or at the very least convince him to abandon this kidnap plot. I'm searching for a way to broach the topic when he looks at me and frowns.

"You can't say a word to Lay," he says. "Not a word."

"Yeah."

"Or to anyone else."

"I get it, bro."

Sean relaxes his grip on the steering wheel.

"This is the boldest thing they've ever done," he says. "And they picked us."

This is my opening.

"Doesn't that bother you? I mean, why would they choose us, the newest members? The youngest members. Why don't Viper and Sidewinder do it themselves? They're combat veterans. They're trained to do this kind of shit. Why us, man?"

"Because they trust us."

"They trust us based on what exactly?"

"So, maybe it's a test. Or maybe he picked us because we live in Astoria. We know the city really well, so there's less chance of getting caught."

"Are you buying all that 'she's the enemy of the people' crap? Seems like Viper's gone off the edge to me. Kidnapping a senator? It's crazy. If we're caught, it's life in prison."

Sean tightens his grip on the wheel again.

"If you're too scared, drop out," he snaps. "I can do it alone."

"I think we both need to drop out. Before we get in too deep. Just talking to Viper about it can get us arrested."

"You shouldn't have joined. You don't believe in the cause."

The comment takes me by surprise. I study my roommate's face for a few moments. There's a cruel sneer etched on it that I've never seen before.

"Maybe you're right. Maybe I just want things to go back to the way they were. Sean, you've changed. I barely know you anymore."

"I've grown up, Robb. I realize now, for the first time, that I have to stand up for what's right. Protecting our freedoms. That's what True Patriots is all about."

"Have you read Austin's bill? Nobody's freedom is at stake."

"Not at first, but give that bitch an inch and she'll come back with another bill. And another. Soon, they'll be going door to door, taking away our guns. Soon, it'll be next to impossible to buy one."

I recognize the words. It's almost verbatim the kind of disinformation that's been spreading in far-right chat rooms. My friend has fallen down a rabbit hole, and it's my job to rescue him.

Somehow.

Another savage silence gnaws at my heart.

"Are you in or out?" he asks suddenly.

"I've got your back," I say in a weak voice.

"Good to hear."

CHAPTER
FOURTEEN
ROBB

HE STANDS OUT, with his tailored gray suit and shiny leather shoes. Not exactly tourist apparel.

Plus, there's the fact that he's Black. A tad unusual for these parts.

The man is in the front of my shop, checking out the new and used bikes – the sleek electric ones, the beach roamers with super-fat tires and the old-school fendered cruisers with their handy baskets.

"Can I help you?" I ask from behind the sales counter.

He doesn't face me right away. Instead, he whistles.

"These prices," he says, examining the tag on a cherry-red electric. "Two grand for a bicycle."

"Well worth it. Lots of steep hills here."

"Yeah, Little San Francisco, they say. Sell many of them?"

"Nah, this is more of a used-bike town. But I get a lot of people looking – like you."

"Been busy?"

"Not really. That starts in late spring. Mostly do repair jobs this time of year."

He turns and I finally see his face. He's maybe 65, with gray sprinkled like powdered sugar in his hair. Dressed like he's headed to a fancy dinner party, with a cornflower silk tie and matching pocket square.

"Sorry, don't mean to take up much of your time. I just have a few questions." He fishes into his breast pocket and flashes a badge.

My knees instantly grow weak. I put my elbows on the counter to steady myself.

"Spencer Williams, FBI. You're Bartholomew Robbins, right?"

"Yeah. Robb, to my friends. You're a little old to be an agent aren't you?"

He smiles and smooths his mustache. "They won't let me retire. Not officially anyway. Like I said, I have a few questions. Mind if we close the store and talk in back? Won't take long."

"Um, okay," I say, watching as he steps over to the front door and reverses the hanging "We're Open" sign.

We sit on a couple of stools in my repair shop, surrounded by an assortment of ailing bikes hanging from hooks. The walls are lined with spare tires and inner tubes. The counters are filled with a jumble of parts from pedals to gears.

I don't bother turning on the overhead fluorescent lights. There's something about the semi-darkness that's soothing.

"Nice business you have," he says, looking around. "Good downtown location."

"You think so?" As a trained observer, he must have seen the homeless man leaning against the wall next to my front door.

"Well, it will be. You know, gentrification and all that. Why bikes?"

"Excuse me?"

"Why did you choose to open a bike shop? I'm just curious."

"Bikes don't pollute, they give you exercise, and they're not very complicated. Besides, I can show up every day in a T-shirt and jeans."

"Makes sense."

"You're not from here."

"Is it that obvious? My wife and I traded Chicago for Cannon Beach a couple of years ago. She runs a small bookstore now, just off the beach."

I don't really want to make small talk with a federal agent, but it's easing my nerves a little.

"Why Oregon? Why not Florida?" He wrinkles his nose. "Florida sucks. Crazy people, high humidity, higher heat. Those 90-90 days. Just awful. Been to the Oregon coast a few times for work. Kinda liked it. You know, the ocean, good coffee and chowder, the whole bit."

"But you're still working cases?"

"Sometimes, when I get a little stir-crazy. But my traveling days are over. Now I only accept the big ones that are close to home. Like this."

"I see." *Here it comes.*

He pulls out a small notebook and a pen. The brown warmth in his eyes drains away and there's nothing but steel left.

"True Patriots," he says. "Heard of them?"

I gulp. "Yeah, sure. Militia group."

"We've been watching them for years. They know it, so they encrypt everything, keep their business secret – except for those ridiculous monthly meetings at the firehouse."

"What does any of that have to do with me?"

He scribbles a note, then looks me square in the eyes. "We've been watching you, too. We know that you and your friend just became members."

"So what? They have a lot of members – a lot of ex-cops like you."

"I was never a cop," he says with a frosty smile. "Why did you join?"

The truthful answer is I joined to protect my friend. And I'm scared to death.

"Sounded like fun," I say, shrugging.

"Does going to prison sound like fun to you? Because everyone stupid enough to join True Patriots may be headed there."

So much for my humor and sarcasm.

"Look, am I under investigation? If so, I'd like a lawyer. And I don't have to answer any more of your questions."

The agent raises a hand and his demeanor softens. "Look, this is strictly informal," he says. "I'm just going to ask for your cooperation."

I fold my arms across my chest and say nothing.

"We understand that True Patriots is planning something very serious. I'd like you to help us stop it before anyone gets hurt."

"I don't know what you're talking about," I say, but I'm a terrible liar and he seems to sense that.

"Mr. Robbins, I'd like you to find out what's going on and report back to me. If you provide valuable information, we can offer you immunity."

"You mean be some kind of informant? I thought you said you've been watching them. You can find out for yourself."

"We don't have a man on the inside. We need your help. We need lead time."

I glare at the dapper man across from me.

"For all I know you're a fraud, working for Viper and just testing my loyalty. And you know what? I wouldn't blame him. How many militias around the country have been infiltrated by undercover agents?"

"You've done some reading."

"You're damn right I have."

"Well, then you know why the militias are being 'infiltrated,' as you say. You've read about the plots being hatched across the country to kill judges, prosecutors and politicians who stand in their way."

"I'm aware."

"Look, I know you're not one of them. You're looking out for your friend, and that's commendable. But if you somehow became involved in one of these plots, you'd both be in a whole lot of trouble."

I shudder because this man just said what I've been thinking for days now – what I've been losing sleep over. But there still must be a way out of this mess without blowing the whistle. *There must be.*

"I'm done talking," I say, burying my trembling fingers under my thighs. "You're hurting my business."

It's an empty claim, but he nods. Placing a business card on the counter, he rises to his feet.

"My personal number is on there," he says. "Call me any time, day or night, if you change your mind."

"Don't hold your breath."

The FBI man looks at me with a measure of sadness.

"Best to keep this chat quiet," he says. "Viper and company won't believe that you turned me down."

CHAPTER
FIFTEEN
ROBB

THE CARD FLIPS in my fingers. Front, back, front, back.

My efforts to persuade Sean to abandon the scheme have failed. If anything, he's more determined than ever to prove himself worthy of True Patriots. He has orders from Viper.

He's in the Twilight Zone but not a lost cause. I know that in my heart. He's not a real militia man. Not yet.

The FBI agent's sudden appearance at my shop was jarring. But the feds apparently only know the militia is plotting something illegal. They lack the information needed to get warrants and raid Viper's command post.

I can cut some kind of a deal. There's still time. I can save the senator and Sean.

I'm sitting in the dark in my repair shop, fretting. My front door bell tinkles and I jump off the stool with a start. I stuff the card in my back pocket as Sean walks in.

"Bro," he says, "did you forget to pay the power bill?"

"Just thinking," I say, getting up to flip the switch.

Tube lights hanging down flicker on and what I see stuns me.

Sean is wearing a camo uniform with a TP shoulder patch. All his curly blond hair is gone, down to the scalp. Shaved off like a boot camp enlistee.

"What the fuck?"

He smiles at my reaction. "Meet the new me."

In just over 30 days, he'd become a convert. A proud skinhead with a uniform and a gun.

"Why?"

"Time to take things more seriously. You should, too. What were you thinking about?"

It's hard to reason after such a jolt, but I try. "The mission."

I'm being cryptic because I fear the FBI man I allowed back here planted listening devices. That's what joining a paranoid extremist group does to you.

"Good," Sean says, looking relieved. "I need your brain power. You've been distracted lately."

"Well, it's not sticking cherry bombs in mailboxes like when we were 14. A lot's at stake."

Sean nods. "Viper contacted me. He wants us to hold the target overnight to make sure we got away clean; that it's safe to come here."

"Figures. We take all the risk. He'll take all the glory."

"Don't look at it like that."

"Sean, open your eyes. What do you think will happen when someone that important goes missing? The whole weight of the government and law enforcement will come down on us. And the local militia will be suspect No. 1."

Now, I've done it. Almost spilled the beans. I really hope there are no bugs back here.

"So what? There won't be a trail leading to us; Viper will make sure of that. He's got our backs."

"And if they kill her? Do you want blood on your hands?" I ask.

"It won't come to that. They're just going to hold onto her until the gun bill fizzles."

"You trust Viper that much?"

"Yeah, I do."

"Well, I don't. Maybe you've been spending too much time over there, hanging out."

"Training. You should try it, you'll learn a few things."

There's a thick silence – a common wall between us these days. All I can do is shrug.

Sean looks at me and grins in an odd way.

"We're going to put her in the basement," he says. "Nobody but you has the key?"

"Yeah, that's right."

"Not even the owner?"

"Just me."

"Perfect. We'll set it up tonight."

———

Two days before the mission.

Sean is out doing his recon or whatever, and I'm nervous as hell.

I knock on Mrs. Wong's door to hand her the day's mail. There's a heavy box from Pottery Barn and several pouches shipped from China, probably some of her tea herbs and ramen noodles.

She smiles as I come into focus. The tea kettle is whistling. It's always demanding her attention.

"Come in, my boy," the old woman says, hustling off in her

slippered semi-shuffle. She quiets the kettle and pours two cups of tea.

"I can't stay," I say, but she's having none of that. She stabs a bony finger at a chair, places the steaming cups on a bare spot on the cluttered kitchen table.

I'm freaking out about the TP plot and can barely think straight. The last thing I need is to have tea with a matchmaker who will probably ask when I'm going to propose to the woman in No. 5. But I have to keep up appearances, so I take a seat.

Mrs. Wong cradles her cup in her wrinkled hands, breathes in the steam. An aroma of seaweed and forest moss fills the air.

"You drink, you like," she says with a wink.

I take a sip and instantly feel calmer. She's like some kind of witch doctor with her various potions.

"You talk to lovely girl?"

"Layla? Not yet," I say. "The time doesn't seem right."

It may never be right.

"Silly boy," she says. "You ask soon. Love fly away, not to return. Understand? *Oooh!*"

Mrs. Wong notices the Pottery Barn box for the first time and springs to her feet. She rips at the cardboard with her fingers like a ravenous wolverine and sticks her head halfway in, emerging with a ceramic lamp and fabric shade.

She scurries off to her bedroom. There's a clatter as she clears a space for her latest purchase. I take a sip of my tea and am about to quietly leave when Mrs. Wong returns with another lamp. A packing slip is taped to the base. At least she's an organized shopaholic.

"Better," she declares. "You send this back, please?"

"Sure, Mrs. Wong." *What else do I have to do, other than clear room in the building for a prisoner?*

"Now you go. Talk to girl."

Layla is going to have to wait. I desperately need to think. I head down the stairs and am about to duck inside my apartment when Aliston pops his head out.

"Robb! Austin will be here Friday night!"

"Cool," I say, trying not to sound flustered.

He steps into the hall wearing what appears to be a black velvet smoking jacket. *Where do you even buy something like that?* He hands me a couple of tickets.

"For you and Layla. Reserved seating," he says proudly.

"Oh, wow. Thanks, dude."

"I'll be there, but I'll be backstage with the VIPs. Been working nonstop on getting everything set up. I think it's going to be the most press Astoria has ever had!"

"I'll definitely try to be there, man."

Aliston's cellphone buzzes and he disappears into his apartment with a thumb's up. "See ya!"

Alone in the lobby, my back slumped against the wall, the first thought I have is who would provide the best alibi: Layla, Aliston or Mrs. Wong?

Good grief. Now I'm thinking like a criminal.

CHAPTER
SIXTEEN
VIPER

WEASEL IS LOOKING at me with turquoise eyes enlarged by Coke-bottle glasses, gauging my reaction.

"Are you fucking kidding me?!"

Instead of cowering when I yell like most of my men, he grins. Flicks his tongue over his lips like a lizard. He's a strange one, my security chief. The short little prick.

He's been keeping tabs on my prized recruit, who's been conspicuously trying to be inconspicuous in casing the building where the kidnapping is about to go down.

Weasel just told me that he easily spotted Hawkeye peering through binoculars and jotting notes in the condo parking lot.

Clumsy at best, especially with security people in town preparing for the senator's visit. Any suspicious characters would undoubtedly be scooped up and questioned. The operation would have to be scuttled out of an abundance of caution.

"Any more good news?"

Weasel peels off his wire-rimmed glasses, wipes the thick lenses with a handkerchief. Without the distortion, his eyes seem small and tired, the flesh around them baggy and pale.

"The secure location is a go," he says in his usual hushed tone. We're outside, in the middle of an empty pasture, but Weasel is ex-CIA and trained to be extremely cautious.

"You're certain?"

"Absolutely."

"And if they come?"

"We'll see vehicles approach more than a mile in any direction."

"What about choppers?"

"Spotters on the roof should be able to give you several minutes' notice. They'll have RPGs if you want to take them out."

"Good to know. What about the building itself?"

"Swept several times. It's clean."

The secure location is an abandoned chemical storage facility on the Oregon side of the Columbia about 40 minutes west of Portland. It was built in the early 1950s, with concrete floors and cinderblock walls.

The property is ringed by an 8-foot-tall chain-link fence with a padlocked gate. Littering the grounds are rusty steel drums that had once held a host of toxins. The state of Oregon is in the process of declaring the site a threat to groundwater and the river. There's no way anyone would want to stop by for a surprise visit. A major selling point.

One of my members owns the wretched place and handed over the keys without hesitation. Even so, I ordered Weasel to check it out. I was taking no chances. This is where the senator will stand trial for her sins, if all goes according to plan.

"Nice work," I tell Weasel. "I guess now we take care of the friend and wait for the call."

"May I ask a question?"

"Sure. What's on your mind?"

"It's obvious that those two have no experience running a high-stakes op. What makes you think they can get the job done?"

I scratch my ear and sigh.

"The risk is all theirs. If it goes right – great. If it goes wrong, well, there's no way those yahoos can pin anything on True Patriots. Their word means nothing. And then, my friend, we proceed to Plan B."

Plan B calls for assassinating the senator. Sniper positioned on a rooftop across from her Portland office. She'll get what she deserves. Right between the eyes.

"Do you want me to keep watching Hawkeye?" Weasel asks.

"Both of them. If they go to the cops or the FBI, I want to know."

"Certainly."

"Anything more on the target's girlfriend?"

"What would you like to know?" Weasel is grinning again. That, coupled with his oversized reptilian eyes, creeps me out.

"Are they lesbian lovers?"

"Used to be," he says with a flicker of disappointment. "Apparently, the good senator is seeking to relight the flame. For political reasons, they've been apart. I believe she is planning to go public as a homosexual after the vote on the bill."

"They're keeping her relationship under wraps so she can muster a few Republican votes?"

"That's the thinking inside her office, according to our source."

"These libs are such hypocrites. What is your read of what will happen if the target simply disappears for a while?"

"If the gun bill is to pass, it's crucial that she rallies public opinion until the vote. It's at a tipping point. She's scheduled to speak on the eve of the Senate vote in Washington. If she can't whip up more enthusiasm, the bill will fail. But that only happens if she merely disappears. If there's evidence of foul play, all bets are off."

"Not to worry," I say. "Our friends across the country will use social media to spread the narrative that Austin disappeared because she couldn't take the heat."

"So, she got out of the kitchen." Weasel issues a bitter laugh that sounds like a small child choking. "Still, better to just eliminate her quickly and be done with it."

"No, she needs to stand trial first. She's betrayed her country."

"Yes, but I would advise you not to screw around. We have local law enforcement under control, but the FBI are no fools."

"It'll be a fast trial, I can assure you. A warning to all the others who would dare to carry her torch. And you'll be shooting the video that will cement our legacy."

"An honor. You didn't ask me about the escape plan."

"For the secure location? Do we need one?"

"Always a good idea."

I smile at the little man with the big brain. "Tell me."

He licks his lips again with that darting tongue. "The warehouse has a basement – an additional storage area. In looking it over, we found a hidden door."

Weasel pauses for dramatic effect, then continues. "It leads to a concrete-lined tunnel that runs some 400 yards north to the river. Apparently, they were doing some illegal dumping for years. The tunnel ends near a small loading dock, hidden by trees."

"Very interesting."

"Indeed. I'll arrange to have a boat waiting."

"In case the feds crash the party?"

"Yes, but also to take us to the rendezvous point."

"Good job."

I watch as a bald eagle glides gracefully overhead. Undoubtedly a patriotic omen.

When I look down, there's only Weasel's back. He's hustling away, eager to resume his surveillance. Seconds later, he fades like a ghost in the low-hanging fog.

The plan to spur America's second revolution is coming together nicely. The fuse has been lit.

CHAPTER
SEVENTEEN
ROBB

IMMENSE PRESSURE is building inside me. It feels like every molecule is going to explode, leaving nothing but fire and ash.

I can't work up the courage to call Williams. Can't work up the courage to go through with the mission either.

It's my job to be the getaway driver, to wait in the stolen van for Sean to force the target out of the condo.

The plan is to smuggle her into the River Vista basement, where she can't be seen or heard. Cuff her to a steel pipe running down one of the brick walls. Take turns checking on her and providing food and water.

We'll both wear masks and gloves, and she'll be blindfolded going in and out of the building. Sean will ditch the van in the woods outside of town.

With any luck, the senator will be in Viper's hands before anyone knows she's gone.

The problem is relying on luck.

"I don't think we're ready," I tell Sean as we're standing in the musty basement. "We should delay."

We've created a makeshift cell. A small cot in a corner with a blanket and pillow. A plastic jug of water and a few Nutri-Grain bars. There's an old shower against the other wall that I was surprised still works. Also, a laundry room-type sink, but no toilet – just a bucket.

"No delays," Sean says firmly. "It's going down tonight. I'll be waiting in the condo, you'll be at the wheel, just like we planned."

"What if her security team gets curious? I mean, they'll be right outside. If she screams …"

"She won't."

"But, what if she does? We don't have a plan for that."

"Look, you're just nervous. Don't worry. I got the layout of the condo from the real estate company. And it'll take less than five minutes to get her down here from there. We're as ready as we'll ever be."

Just my luck to be teamed with a master war game strategist and newly crowned champion shooter.

Sean draws his Glock from the back of his jeans, where it's been concealed under a loose cotton shirt.

"If anyone gets in our way," he says, "they'll be sorry."

———

There are only a few hours left.

Panicked, I reach out to Layla, hoping she can brainstorm a way out of this mess.

We meet at a dive bar on the east side of town. Men cluster around blue-felt pool tables and old-timers drink $2 Rainier drafts as Bob Seger belts out "Fire Down Below." Nobody pays any attention to us, which is good.

Sharing a booth paneled with knotty pine, she sees the desperation in my eyes.

"Talk to me, Robb. What's bothering you?"

I squeeze my head with both hands as if to push out the words.

"I'm in trouble, Lay. Big trouble."

She reaches across the table, putting her smooth hand over mine. "Whatever it is, you can tell me."

I look into her gold-infused eyes and see nothing but compassion. Still, I hesitate. I'm about to violate Sean's trust for the first time in my life.

"It's the militia," I say. "They've given us a mission."

"What kind of mission?"

"It's crazy. You won't believe it. You'll think I'm making it up."

"You've never lied to me," she says, squeezing my hand. "You're trembling. Tell me what's going on."

"You have to promise not to tell a soul."

"I promise."

My throat is dry as a desert. I realize we didn't grab drinks when we came in. Too much weighing on my overloaded brain.

"How 'bout a drink first? I think I need one ... or three."

She nods and I get up and grab us a couple of Rainiers and tequila shots. I down the shot right after sitting down. That reminds me of Talisman, which doesn't help.

"C'mon, Robb, the suspense is killing me."

I look around to make sure nobody is near but still lower my voice to a whisper.

"We're supposed to kidnap Senator Austin when she visits Astoria tonight. Hand her over to Viper, the leader."

Layla jumps back against the knotty pine as if shot out of a cannon.

"Oh my God, are you serious? What will they do to her?"

"Hold some kind of kangaroo trial. They're trying to stop her gun bill. They're spooked that it may pass."

"Baby, are they going to kill her?"

"I don't know. I mean, I hope not. Shit, I don't know."

Still stunned, she shakes her head. "Why you two? You just joined."

"I've been wondering about that. All I can figure is that Sean and me aren't being watched like the others. We're too new. Or maybe we're just more expendable."

A familiar fire fills Layla's eyes. "Just get out now, both of you. Refuse to go through with it. Go to the police."

"Sean won't do that. He's brainwashed. He's told me several times that if I pull out, he'll do it himself. And if I blow the whistle, I'll be sending my best friend to prison."

"If you don't, you'll go to prison, too. Jesus, Robb. A man from the FBI came to see me yesterday. He was asking about you. I tried to tell you about it, but you weren't around."

This can't get any worse. I pull the card from my pocket and place it on the table.

"Was his name Spencer Williams?"

"Yeah, that's it. What's it all about?"

"He wants me to be an informant. He knows True Patriots is up to something big, but he doesn't know what."

"What did you tell him?"

"Nothing. He surprised me in my shop and I kinda told him to fuck off." I start squeezing my head again.

Layla is deep in thought, her brow wrinkled. After several tense minutes, she offers a plan.

"Tell Sean the FBI contacted you, that they're on to the kidnapping.

Show him the card. That should convince him to back off. If not, you have to save yourself."

"Sean's my bud, Lay," I say. "I'll do what you just said, but I can't give up on him. I can't ever abandon him."

I don't bother explaining why. She's heard the teenage treasure hunt story before.

Across the table, Layla's tough facade crumbles. She starts to cry.

I get up and sit next to her, holding her body as it convulses.

"It'll be okay," I say, but I don't believe it.

Not at all.

CHAPTER
EIGHTEEN
ALEX

ASTORIA'S LIBERTY Theatre sits in the heart of the historic downtown district, surrounded by restaurants, galleries and gift shops. Its oldtimey marque has been tastefully preserved and the interior is immaculate – red fabric seats and a stage flanked by ornate columns and grand, Baroque-style arches. A miniature Carnegie Hall.

I picked it because it's close to Mandy's gallery – less than four blocks. Wes liked it because the optics were good for a televised town hall-style forum.

Tickets were reserved for 600 people. Metal detectors were set up in the lobby, a security measure prompted by death threats over my bill. They'd catch anyone bringing in a firearm, but I found the notion of being gunned down at a gun-control event to be mind-warping.

My security people had advised me not to hold the event. Too risky. When I persisted, they asked me to wear a bullet-proof vest "out of an abundance of caution." They said nobody would notice. It would be under my clothes. I thanked them for their concern but refused. I'd come this far. It wasn't a time to show fear.

That's what the crazies want.

So, here I am on a Friday night in March. In the wings, waiting to be introduced by Clara Johnson, one of the anchors for Portland's highest-rated TV news station. A Barbie doll blonde in a pink dress, she seems perfect for her line of work: Talking into a camera with a glossed perma-smile.

She tells the crowd my story. Uses the familiar words "hero" and "crusader." Ends with, "And it's my great pleasure to introduce your senator, Alex Austin."

I step out to applause and see mostly smiling faces, which calms my nerves a bit. I scan the front rows and don't see Mandy. Maybe she's somewhere in the back, or watching at home.

Please be watching.

"Thank you, Clara," I say as I replace her at the lectern, looking frumpy by comparison in my black pant suit. I open a slim vinyl binder and begin reading my prepared remarks without the aid of a teleprompter. I've written "From your heart!" on top of the first page.

"We're in a fight, ladies and gentlemen. A fight for the health of our great nation. We have witnessed how gun violence in this country has spiraled out of control, how despite the rising toll of innocent victims, despite all the bloodshed, we have actually stepped backwards in terms of preventing these tragedies. There have been more than 4,000 mass shootings since Sandy Hook in 2012. Let me repeat that: *four thousand.*

"As most of you know, I survived a shooting that claimed the lives of several of my co-workers and 24 children. Elementary school children. They could have been your kids. Or your neighbor's kids. They were innocent, but still they were gunned down in cold blood with an assault rifle. By an 18-year-old who was mentally ill, who had a history of disturbing incidents in the year before the massacre, including shooting the family dog. He amassed an arsenal, but he shouldn't have been allowed to do so. He waved red flags at us, but the laws we have on the books didn't allow us to act.

"The Mass Shooting Prevention Act changes that. Finally. It will prevent the sale of assault-style weapons that should only be in the hands of our police and our military. It will raise the minimum age to purchase a firearm to 21 and close loopholes that allow some purchasers to avoid background checks. The law also prohibits the sale of guns to persons with a history of serious mental illness. It could have made a difference in Marsten. It could have saved lives – young lives."

The words are greeted with sustained applause, prompting me to stop for a few moments.

"I'm not asking for the impossible," I say. "This isn't tilting at windmills. We've banned assault rifles before in this country. We can do it again. Only this time, we need to get the job done. We need to also ban high-capacity ammo clips. We need to do more and better screening. We need to create a smarter purchaser database that the FBI can use to protect us, and we have to invest more in screening of the dark web to crack down on domestic terrorists plotting mass shootings.

"The time for complacency is over. The time to act is now. Nobody wants to take away anyone's lawfully purchased guns. Hunters and sportsmen can rest easy. But we must – we absolutely must – look to the future. We must do all we can to prevent more massacres. Thank you. I'll take questions from the audience now, and then the press."

The podium is whisked away and the stage quickly transforms. Suddenly I'm sitting in a padded chair across from the moderator, a small round table and two water glasses between us. We're both holding microphones.

Johnson reads one of the index cards in her lap.

"Our first question is from Lindsey Buckman of Astoria. Go ahead, Lindsey."

Buckman, who is standing in a carpeted aisle, is handed a mic by an aide. She identifies herself as a mother of two who works for a mortgage company in town.

"My question is this: I appreciate your effort, but it seems doomed. The NRA is too strong. The country is too divided. How can you possibly win?"

If I hadn't been hearing that kind of sentiment every day for months and months, I'd have been discouraged by the zinger of an opening question. Instead, it makes me smile.

"We *will* win, Lindsey. We'll win because the grip the NRA has on Congress has never been weaker. It's a tired old organization rife with division and corruption, and its days are numbered. They are today's tobacco lobby. We'll win also because the American people are with us. Polls show a large majority favor reasonable gun control measures and the Mass Shooting Prevention Act is built on common sense."

"Well said, senator," Johnson tells me under her breath. "The next question is from Robert Tillman of Seaside. Go ahead, please."

Tillman, who is wearing a suit for the occasion and identifies himself as a real estate broker, thanks me for saving lives at McReedy Elementary. He has four young kids of his own and lives in fear of them being shot.

"I've come to realize that nobody is really safe from gun violence. Even here on the quiet North Coast. We have to do something. We have to act. So, I guess I don't really have a question. I just want to say, thank you, Senator Austin."

I glance at the sideline behind the curtain and see Wes beaming. Even Henderson, clutching his laptop, seems pleased.

And then Rory Bellwether grabs the mic.

"I've seen your bill," he says in disgust. "It's blatantly unconstitutional."

He pauses, but I'm caught off-guard and can't muster an immediate response.

"Not only are you going to take away our guns," he continues, "but you're going to spy on us as well. Create a secret database. What you're doing, senator, is treasonous."

The crowd is murmuring as I gather myself for a rebuttal. Bellwether identified himself only as a "local businessman," but I remember him now from the acidic emails he sent to my offices in Portland and Washington. And the equally caustic letters to the papers.

"Mr. Bellwether, I think we should tell the audience that you make your living selling guns. In fact, doesn't Rory's Guns & More sell the most assault rifles in Oregon?"

"Yeah, but you want to put me out of business. It's … un-American."

"Un-American? Tell me something, Mr. Bellwether," I say, rising to my feet. "How does it feel knowing that several of your guns were found in the McReedy killer's trailer? What is it like profiting off sales to a mass murderer?"

There are audible gasps. People in the crowd are glaring at the gun merchant.

"I support the laws we have on the books today," he seethes. "Not what you have in your bill. That's overkill. Totally unnecessary."

"Do you support selling military-grade guns to terrorists?"

"No, but ..."

"That's good to hear, because the Mass Shooting Prevention Act is all about preventing dangerously mentally ill people, felons and terrorists, foreign and domestic, from being able to get their hands on those weapons – the kind most commonly used in shooting sprees because they inflict the most damage."

Bellwether's ruddy face gets redder. "Stop taking away our guns!"

"You have nothing to worry about, sir. Just do your part and we can finally do something about the plague of gun violence infecting our nation."

The audience applauds and I see Wes wiping imaginary sweat from his brow.

After the gun store owner, the rest of the questions go smoothly. An hour or so later, the moderator thanks the groups and individuals that made the event possible. There's a break as the audience clears out and reporters move to a designated area by the stage for the presser.

I'm surprised to see the Fox emblem on one of the cameras. I wonder how the network's conservative on-air personalities in New York City are reacting to my speech. I doubt they covered it live, but I am absolutely certain that they are showing Bellwether's angry statement – without any of my response.

The podium returns and I thank the press for coming. I don't give another speech, just invite the reporters' questions.

One of the Washington Post reporters who covers the Capitol is first.

"Only four Republicans are publicly backing your bill, senator. It doesn't appear to have the votes needed to overcome a filibuster. What is your response?"

I shrug. "Five weeks ago, no Republicans supported the bill. I'd say we're making progress."

"But if you can't get more Republicans to sign on …"

"Then it will fail. But there are several days before the vote and the political landscape is evolving in our favor. The polls show that. Doing nothing to control gun violence is like doing nothing to prevent global warming. It's simply not an option. I believe strongly that the Senate will find a way to come together on this vital issue."

The journalist from The New York Times is next.

"What elements of your bill do you consider essential?" she asks.

"All of it," I say. "If we water it down, it won't make a difference, and we owe it to all the victims of gun violence in this country to demand real change."

"But what if the holdouts in the Senate insist that the assault weapons ban be dropped? Can you live with that?"

"Funny that you would use the word 'live.' It's really the point, isn't it? In the past six weeks there have been a dozen mass shootings in a dozen different states. Assault weapons were used in those attacks. We can't allow this to continue."

I feel I'm holding my ground, thanks in part to a subsequent series of softball questions about my personal motivations. But then a tall, wiry man steps up to the mic. He's wearing round glasses and his short blond hair is gelled into place.

"Benson Buckley, Fox News," he declares with a certain unfounded arrogance. "The database you want to create would enable the federal government to spy on every gun owner in America, isn't that true?"

I look over at Wes, who's grown pale. A misstep here would be catastrophic.

"There's already a database," I say after a few moments. "Every lawful gun owner is in it because of routine background checks.

There's very little controversy about that. What I seek to accomplish is to give the government, specifically the FBI, the ability to screen more effectively for disturbed individuals or terrorists who may be planning attacks."

Buckley smirks. "But in order to do so, wouldn't that new screening amount to spying on millions of law-abiding Americans?" "Absolutely not. Just as we did during the war on terror, and still do, we are only looking for bad actors – for example, tying web chatter about a plot to shoot up a school with a recent gun purchase. For the first time, we'd have all the tools to stop mass shootings before they happen. Before innocent lives are lost."

More smirking. "Senator, isn't your bill just a prelude to seizing guns? Isn't that your true goal? You said words to that effect in an interview two years ago. I can read it to you, if you'd like."

He's not all wrong.

I did a TV interview a few weeks after the McReedy bloodbath during which I said every assault rifle in the hands of civilians needed to be melted down to scrap. It was trauma-fueled hyperbole, and I was imagining the nation's biggest gun buyback program, not "seizing" weapons, but Fox's talking heads seldom bother with context.

As Buckley waves a sheet of paper, I grip the podium. I feel like yelling at this clown, but I push those emotions away.

"Despite what your network says, I fully support the rights of hunters and sportsmen to own rifles, as well as the right of citizens to obtain carry permits for personal protection. And nowhere in this bill will you see any reference to taking those guns away."

Preventing yet another Buckley parry, Johnson leans in. She ends the news conference with a practiced smile.

"Thank you for coming," she says. "That's all the time we have."

———

It's after 8 p.m. when we leave the theater. Wes is amped, certain we'll get the political boost we need. Maybe convince those last GOP senators.

We cross the rain-soaked street to a restaurant with a marble-topped bar where I order a chilled pinot grigio. He orders a double Jameson neat.

He checks his phone and slaps his knee. "Yes!"

"What?"

"Senator Haskell is on board. He watched your remarks and decided to throw in."

"Haskell, of Iowa?" I ask, dumbfounded.

"*Republican* senator from Iowa. He was on the fence, but I thought he'd cave to the gun lobby. This is great news."

"How many more converts do we need?"

"Five, assuming the Dems fall in line."

It was Wes who devised the strategy that got a handful of moderate Republicans to break ranks. The first cracks in the dam. We slipped in a provision in an early version of the bill that revoked the business licenses of every gun store in the country that had sold a weapon used in a mass shooting.

If cast into law, the provision would have shuttered more than a thousand stores from coast to coast. Wes and I used that as a bargaining chip, agreeing to delete the language in exchange for public support. It worked beautifully, allowing me to claim modest bipartisan support in the press.

"Is it really possible?" I ask. "Passage?"

Wes squeezes my shoulder. "We've only got a few days before the vote, but, yes, it's possible. We've got to take your show on the road, generate buzz the old-fashioned way."

"Where to?"

"Every state with a mass shooting this year and a senator who still claims to be undecided. The NRA wields its power in the dark, but we'll do it in front of the TV cameras. After tonight, there's no doubt: You're a force of nature."

"Hardly. All I really proved tonight was that I can spar with far-right lackeys."

I glance at my watch. Wes, noticing, stops smiling.

"There's nothing I can say to change your mind, is there?"

"I have to see her, even if it's just for a little while."

"I get it. I'll drop you off, then I'll be at the hotel with Henderson, crunching numbers and making calls."

"Thanks."

"Alex?"

"Yes?"

"For what it's worth, I'm sorry. I hope it works out between you two."

I nod and check for messages from Mandy on my phone. There aren't any, which means she's still willing to see me. There's a chance to set things right.

"Let's go," I say. "She's waiting."

CHAPTER
NINETEEN
VIPER

WEASEL GOES IN first, that creepy grin plastered on his face.

I follow a few minutes later, see my security man in a corner of the gallery, ogling opulently framed nudes.

It's minutes to closing and I hasten the process by locking the glass door behind me. I slowly work my way toward the target, pretending to be an art lover, which I definitely am not. Especially queer art, which this place seems to specialize in.

The redhead I recognize from Weasel's surveillance photos as Mandy Malone greets us warmly from behind a small counter. Her hair is up and she's in a beige long-sleeve sweater dress with brown ankle boots.

"Welcome," she says. "Let me know if you have any questions."

I almost laugh. She thinks she's seeing her lady friend tonight, but she's got a big surprise coming. They both do.

We've kept our backs to her, but out of the corner of my eye I see Weasel slipping on his mask, edging closer to the counter. I pull mine out of my back pocket and find a spot by a floating wall where I can see her but not be seen.

Weasel is reaching in his pocket and walking backwards. He's just a few feet from Malone now.

I watch in admiration as Weasel suddenly wheels around. The woman's eyes grow wide.

She manages one scream before he plunges a hypodermic needle in her thigh.

"What th--?"

She collapses in a heap. The knockout drug worked even faster than I thought.

I check the front windows, assure myself that nobody outside heard or saw anything.

"All quiet," I tell Weasel, who is staring at the drugged woman's breasts. His little hands twitch, like he's considering fondling her. "Focus, man."

Our Blazer with borrowed plates is waiting by the back door.

I step into the alley, make sure it's all clear, then open the SUV's back hatch. We carry her out and stuff her in, zip-tied and gagged.

"How long will she be out?" I ask.

"Five or six hours. She'll have a headache, but that's about it."

"I won't ask how you know so much about this sort of thing."

"Lots of practice. Black ops. The Company does it all the time."

"Figures. Let's take her to the secure location. We may need her to convince the senator not to try anything foolish. Are you sure there are no security cameras in the gallery?"

"Zero," Weasel says with confidence. "And none on the street."

If Hawkeye and Echo botch their end of the mission tonight, the plan is to dump this lady back in the gallery before she comes to. We go back inside and Weasel pries open the register, snatches some cash and checks. I pull a couple of the most expensive paintings off the walls. We make it look like a robbery, just in case.

We put the art in the back seat, pull off our masks and drive off calm as can be.

"Have you decided what to do with her after the trial?" Weasel asks.

I can tell he's thinking that letting her go is too risky, even if she never saw our faces or heard our voices.

"Not yet, but there's plenty of steel drums out there we can put her in."

"And they sink rather nicely."

"That they do."

We both laugh.

Not a single police siren pierces the chilled night.

CHAPTER
TWENTY
ALEX

MANDY LIVES IN a townhouse with a pretty view of the Columbia that's part of a newish cluster development just off the Astoria Riverwalk.

I've only been inside once, after we'd been forced apart for political expediency. She had realized her dream of opening a gallery, began hanging out with local artists and putting down roots.

In the summer, a trolly laden with tourists regularly passes by, clanging its bell at every stop. But it's the last day of winter and the track imbedded in the boardwalk is dormant. The waterfront seems deserted. The only sound is the distant barking of irritated sea lions.

My heart aches. I miss her so much.

Will this be the end for us or a new beginning? I have no idea. I only know that I am chock full of regret. It'll take a lifetime to make amends for the hurt I've caused, but I'm willing to try. Starting now.

For the first time since the election, I don't care what anyone says about us. I don't care about the polling data or the blizzard of scornful social media posts that seems inevitable. We can weather anything as long as we're together. I know that now.

As our Escalade pulls into the condo complex, Wes is unusually quiet. Or maybe just feeling guilty. I can't tell which.

I show him my phone – an admittedly weak reassurance.

"I'll call if I need a ride back to the hotel or whatever," I say, drawing a nod. "Thank you."

"For what?"

"For this."

"You're being awfully dramatic, Alex."

"Yeah, suppose so." I look through the back window, see the black sedan with my two bodyguards idling nearby. "Please keep them at a discreet distance."

"They've been told."

"What time's the flight to D.C. tomorrow?"

"Quarter to seven, I'm afraid. The president is speaking to the press about gun violence in the late afternoon, and you need to be at his side, offering solutions."

"Fortunately, I have a few," I say, sliding the phone into my bag.

I open the door and stand on the damp pavement, feeling cool mist massage my face like tiny fingers.

Leaning in, I stare at Wes for a moment.

"We're almost at the finish line. Win or lose, we've given it our all."

He gives me his lopsided grin, minus the usual sarcasm.

"When the bill passes and you're on the cover of Time, remember the little people."

"How can I not? You're always demanding credit."

Smiling, I walk through the mist to Mandy's condo.

I know I have the right place. There's a wreath hanging on the door dotted with baby pine cones and miniature ceramic mermaids in different colors. She's always loved mermaids.

Knocking, I turn to wave.

The Escalade is already gone.

CHAPTER
TWENTY-ONE
ROBB

TIME'S UP.

I find Sean in his room, doing bicep curls with 25-pound dumbbells. He snagged the weights for free from a woman on his route who was dumping all of her cheating boyfriend's possessions.

Sean had never cared much about physical fitness before, but now he's borderline obsessed. Viper has tailored a fitness plan for him that includes protein shakes and twice-daily workouts.

I mocked it at first, but now I see the results. His pleasant pudginess is gone. He's leaner and stronger than ever.

He's morphing into a hardcore militia man before my eyes, but I can't just let my friend slip into the void. I steady myself to try to reason with him.

I show Sean the FBI man's card. Tell him Williams is on to True Patriots. Plead with him to call off the mission. Argue that allegiance to Viper isn't worth life in prison.

A stony silence follows that gives me hope. Makes me think I've finally gotten through. But I'm wrong about that.

"You don't have to go," he says in an icy tone. "If you don't have the balls for it, just stay outta my way."

Thirty minutes later, I'm in the van, behind the wheel. Parked in the alley behind the condo complex just as we'd planned. For whatever reason, I'm standing by him, about to become a kidnapper and a hunted man.

I'm in deep. Too damn deep.

Sean is inside with his gun, having forced the rear door with relative ease. It's a tense waiting game now.

I stare out the windshield at the river, see a row of cargo ships anchored nearby, illuminated like Christmas floats.

My window is rolled down and I hear the rumble of a large vehicle approaching on the other side of the building. The target has arrived, right on time.

I think of Layla and the real possibility that I'll never see her again, and my eyes grow moist. I never even told her that I loved her.

"I'm sorry," I say under my breath.

Then I hear knocking.

CHAPTER
TWENTY-TWO
ALEX

NOBODY ANSWERS right away, so I knock again – harder.

The door isn't closed.

Pressure from my hand causes it to slowly open, revealing a slice of the living room. She's not there, but there's music playing and the lights are on.

"Hi! It's me!"

I step inside the tiled entry and look around.

"Mandy? Where are you?"

She must be in the back of the condo, getting ready for my visit. That thought makes me happy, fills me with hope. I close the door, but when I turn around, a man in a black ski mask is in front of me.

Aiming a pistol at my head.

"Scream and you die," he says.

Before I can say anything, he plasters a piece of silver duct tape across my mouth. Then he locks the front door.

In my mounting terror, I realize how foolish I'd been to insist that my bodyguards stay out of sight.

"Put these on," the masked man says, handing me handcuffs. I struggle to catch my breath but do what he wants.

As Mandy's favorite country station plays bizarrely in the background, he looks at me intently. I can see hate in his eyes.

What has he done to Mandy? What does he want with me?

My knees wobble, causing me to lean heavily against a blue velvet sofa. The room is starting to spin.

"Cellphone," he says. "Give it to me."

I can't think straight enough to respond, prompting him to grunt. He snatches my bag away, starts rummaging through it. Finds the phone, stuffs it in his back pocket.

The gunman is wearing faded Levi's, white basketball shoes and a hooded gray sweatshirt with nothing on it. He's about 5-foot-10 and lean. Seems young, but wields that gun like a pro.

"Let's go, out the back," he barks.

He presses the barrel of the gun between my shoulder blades and pushes me through the living room into the kitchen. I'm woozy, though, and slam into a granite counter, which knocks me to my knees.

Swearing, he pulls me up.

Have I interrupted a robbery? Maybe Mandy has been targeted by art thieves.

And then the ghastly face of the Marsten shooter hits me like a bomb.

Bobby Crane gives me a horrible wink. Half of his face is gone, leaving only skull.

Some hero you are.

I try to shut him out, but it's no use.

Some hero.

Tears start streaming down my cheeks. My legs stop working.

The man in the mask cusses again. He grabs me under my left arm, drags me to the back door.

It opens and I catch a glimpse of a white van, its rear doors open. Around me, the kitchen is swirling in oddly shaped ovals like some kind of demented carnival ride.

My eyes close.

Go to sleep, hero. Haw!

"Help me get her in."

"What did you do to her?"

"Nothing. I think she fainted."

There are two of them. One seems scared. I'm outside in the cold.

Hero, hero, hero.

That's my last thought.

Before everything goes dark.

CHAPTER
TWENTY-THREE
ROBB

THIS IS INSANE. It's 9:25 on a Friday night, and I'm in the back of a stolen van looking at an unconscious woman who's gagged and handcuffed.

A powerful woman. A United States senator who is very much in the news and can't simply disappear for a few days without sounding alarms.

Sean stares at me, sizing me up. There's no hiding my emotions from him. He's had me figured out since Mrs. Burns' class in third grade.

"This is a good thing," he says. "Makes it easier."

"How did it go inside?"

"Piece of cake."

Sean tosses me an iPhone in a green plastic case and smiles. "Dumb bitch had it on."

Opening her messages, I see the name I'm looking for, Westley Matthews, at the top. I feel sweat forming on my forehead but force myself to concentrate.

I scroll through a few texts to get a sense of their conversational style, then type.

So great to see her!

I'll be spending the night.

Text you in the morning.

Looking over my shoulder, Sean nods.

"Send it. Should buy us some time. Let's go before her security team decides to do a perimeter check."

I start easing the van out of the alley. Sean points at the river, and I pull into a quiet spot.

Without saying a word, he gets out and takes a look around before flinging the senator's phone deep into the river.

That reminds me. I pull out the burner phone, make the dreaded call.

"Talk to me," Viper says.

"We have her."

"I'll be in touch."

I'm busy checking all the van's mirrors as Sean climbs back in. It's Friday night, but it's the off-season tourist-wise and we're several blocks from the nearest bar.

"How's it looking?" he asks.

"Quiet," I say, a bit surprised. "I made the call. He knows."

"Good." Sean looks in the back, sees Austin's body twitch. "Let's go. She'll be awake in a few minutes."

We wind our way to the apartment building, avoiding the busiest streets. I park the van in front of the River Vista, quietly open the rear doors. Sean has already rolled our captive in a red-and-gold carpet – one of his eBay resale items.

Soon, we're looking like mobsters, carrying the rug down a set of concrete stairs on the building's east side to the basement. At least we won't have to deal with the always curious Mole People.

I unlock the steel door and we drop the rug near our makeshift cell.

"Put your mask on," Sean tells me. He unrolls the rug with his sneakered foot.

Austin tumbles out. Her eyes are closed and her skin is chalky. She looks dead.

"Jesus," I mutter. "It was, like, less than five minutes."

"She's fine," Sean says, giving her a shove.

He's right. She comes to with a cough. Her eyes flutter open and grow wide at the sight of the two of us, looking sinister in our black masks. The gun is back in Sean's hand.

"Don't do anything stupid," he warns. "Try to escape or make any noise and you'll be sorry. Nod if you understand."

She bows her head and looks at me, but I have to turn away. *This isn't who I am.*

Sean isn't done.

"I have no problem strangling you, rolling you back up in that rug and dumping it in the fucking ocean. Understand?"

Another nervous nod.

I don't know what's more horrifying: kidnapping a prominent politician for a band of radicalized whackos or watching my best friend turn into a despicable human being.

Standing behind him, I shake my head. The real militia men are coming. Viper and Sidewinder. What will they do to her?

I'm in too deep.

"Dumping the wheels," Sean says, handing me the gun. I'm surprised by how much it weighs fully loaded.

"Use it if you have to."

The door closes and suddenly I'm alone with a scared senator. She's shaking but I can see strength in her eyes.

It's really happening. My life, all my wishes and dreams, they're crumbling. Is any friend worth such a sacrifice? Then I picture the Sean of just a few months ago and try to steel myself.

I pour some water into a plastic cup and peel back her gag. She takes a couple of gulps.

"Thanks," she rasps.

"Are you hungry?" I ask, waving an apple-cinnamon breakfast bar.

She shakes her head, nervously looks around. "Do you know who I am?"

There's no point in lying. "I do."

"So, you know they'll come looking for me. They probably already are. More cops than you've ever seen."

I nod, saying nothing.

"If you need money …"

"This isn't a robbery."

"What is it?"

"Something worse."

The words hit her like a slap, and I instantly regret causing her more pain.

"It's better that we don't talk," I say.

"There's still time to get out of this. Just let me go, before your friend comes back."

"I can't do that."

"You don't want to kidnap a senator, trust me. They'll shoot to kill. And if you're lucky enough to survive, you'll never get out of prison."

For a few moments, I consider doing what she wants. Let her simply walk out the door. Tell Sean she escaped. Make up some kind of story. But then how long would we have before the feds scooped us up? If we ran, we'd be hunted by both the FBI and Viper and his thugs.

Every scenario racing through my head ended in prison. Or a bullet in the back.

I look deep into the captive's praying eyes.

Then I put the gag back on and cuff her to the pipe.

CHAPTER
TWENTY-FOUR
ALEX

DESPITE ALL THE threats I've received since taking office –
the ones graphically depicting my imminent demise included – I
was never scared. It all seemed so abstract, like an out-of-body
experience. So absurd, in a macabre way.

Death by dismemberment? *Really?*

I was never truly scared. Until now.

Masked men are holding me prisoner at gunpoint in a windowless
basement, like out of some horror movie. I'm sitting in shadow,
chained to a pipe.

The only light comes from a single naked bulb hanging from a
wire over a grimy wash basin that is well out of reach. I look around
and see a jumble of used furniture and household items – dressers,
tables, lamps and bookcases – that fills half the space. There's a
plastic kiddie pool decorated with dinosaurs leaning against a wall,
and next to that an old reel mower and some canoe oars.

They've set me up with a small cot and a blanket, I see. A bucket
for a bathroom.

How long are they planning to keep me here? What did that man, the nicer one, mean by "something worse?"

My mind reels. I'm alone at the moment, locked in this terrible space. I listen for sounds. A passing car, a dog's bark. I hear nothing. Nothing at all. I remember only the van and passing out. I could be anywhere.

My arms tremble as a cold panic rises within me. There's a sudden noise like radio static that makes me turn my head.

A pale figure appears, wearing a flannel shirt shredded with bullet holes.

Bobby Crane gives me a ghoulish, half-skeletal grin.

There she is. The big hero.

I fight back tears, swearing at my show of weakness. I'm a survivor, goddamnit! I'll make it through this somehow.

Close your eyes, hero. Fainting is what you do best.

"Fuck off! Leave me alone!"

A key turns in the lock and my demon disappears. I take a deep breath as the door opens.

It's the man with the trace of kindness in his eyes. The one who hesitated after I warned him. He's my best chance, but I can't persuade him with a gag on.

I make loud murmuring sounds and he comes over. Peels off the tape.

"What?"

"I'm hungry now."

He opens the wrapper of a breakfast bar, puts the food in my newly freed hand.

I take a bite, conjur up a fake smile. I'm not hungry. I just need to try to convince him to help me.

"Is this about the gun bill?" I ask, and he looks startled but says nothing. "If it is, what you're doing won't work. They'll just delay the vote."

He shrugs. "That's up to them. Our part is nearly over."

"Who is 'them?' Who are you working for?"

"Just eat, or I'll put the gag back on."

I finish the bar and look around again. Judging by the old cedar beams and spider-webbed Douglas fir floor boards above, this is likely a residential building, maybe a century old. Glancing at the pile of second-hand furniture, I notice that a couple have price tags. Not exactly a torture dungeon, thank God.

"How am I supposed to sleep with you chaining me to this pipe?" I ask. "I can't exactly lie down on your cot over there, can I?"

He looks at me and actually rolls his eyes. So strange.

"Crap, sorry. I'll figure something out."

"You seem too nice to be mixed up in this."

"Appearances can be deceiving."

"That's true, but no, you're a nice guy, deep down. I can tell."

I watch as he puts the gun down by the sink. *He doesn't like to hold it. He's my guy all right.*

My thoughts go to those death threats. I need to keep him engaged, figure things out. Buy myself some time.

"You know, I get a lot of threats. I guess it comes with the territory if you're as outspoken as I am. But there's one that stands out. This guy really got specific. I mean, even more than usual. How I'd be held to account when I returned to the state, put on trial for my sins."

The masked man is listening. That's good.

"It was so specific, my chief of staff referred it to the Capitol Police and Secret Service. They told me it came from the leader of a militia group, right here in Oregon. They asked local authorities to look into it, and they reported back that this man, a former Marine, was merely engaging in constitutionally protected free speech. It was all just a violent fantasy. Can you believe that?"

"You talk too much."

"This militia leader doesn't get arrested, just a verbal reprimand from the sheriff, so he doubles down. Sends me another letter, this time telling me how much he looked forward to putting a bullet between my eyes. He goes by the name Viper. Ring a bell?"

The man blanches, then steps over. Kneeling inches from my face, he gives an unblinking stare.

"I'm not really one of them," he whispers.

So, now I know. True Patriots is behind this.

An armed extremist group has abducted me in a scheme to stop my bill. Other nut jobs had plotted to snatch Gretchen Whitmer, the Michigan governor, but the FBI stopped the militia before anything happened. Some folks thought it was all bluster, nothing serious. But I knew better. I knew it was a matter of time. And now here I am.

Before I can say anything, the door opens again. It's the other one. The cruel one.

"I heard talking," he says sternly. "Why isn't she gagged?"

"I just gave her food."

The other man rips off a length of duct tape and slaps it over my mouth with such force I fall against the wall, banging my head.

"No more chats," he tells his friend.

To me, he says, "Keep quiet, traitor, and you may survive the night."

Traitor. This one's a true believer.

They turn out the light and leave me in total darkness. Guess I'll not be enjoying the cot tonight.

I'm in the clutches of a militia seeking vengeance, but all I can think of is Mandy and how badly I've screwed things up – again.

When the nicer one returns, I'll ask if she's safe.

CHAPTER
TWENTY-FIVE
ROBB

IT'S THE WORST day of my life. Also, the longest.

Viper got word to Sean before dawn that he's sending someone to pick up the target, but there are security concerns and the transfer can't be made until midnight.

That means more time holding a woman captive, more time keeping up appearances, while at any moment cops with guns could flood the River Vista.

It doesn't help that Sean keeps reminding me not to tell Layla about the senator in the basement.

I bring the mail to Mrs. Wong's apartment, trudging up the stairs. My head is filled with terrible visions of prison cells. Steel toilets and cinderblock walls. Lecherous inmates. Sadistic guards. A monstrous montage from all the B movies I've ever seen.

Her door flings open before I reach the landing.

"Come in, come in," she says, urging me inside with a crooked arm.

We sit at the kitchen table after she sweeps empty delivery boxes and envelopes onto the floor. Within seconds, a hot cup of tea appears in front of me. Lavender and mint.

I don't have time for this nicety, or whatever it is. I need to be shielding the senator from Sean's worst impulses. I can't let him hurt her. That can't also be on my conscience.

I'm tangled in my thoughts and don't immediately notice Mrs. Wong staring at me in a studious way.

"You are far away, my son," she says. "What troubles you?"

I'm on the brink of blowing everything. Arousing an old lady's suspicions. The opposite of what I came here to do. Jesus.

"Nothing," I lie, forcing a smile.

Mrs. Wong points to a dozen white carnations with pink fringe in a smoky gray vase next to the sink. She smiles, creating waves of wrinkles that make her look like a Shar Pei puppy.

"From your girl. Flowers in winter. So lovely. She tell me she worried about you."

The last thing I need is Layla going around expressing her fears. Not when the feds are about to launch a massive manhunt that will tear this town apart.

"I'm fine, really."

I look at her expecting to see disbelief, but instead see only a sudden sadness.

"Is anything the matter, Mrs. Wong?"

She nods. "My sister wants me to leave. Live with her in that very big house."

"Why does she want you to move? You love it here."

I can see the shimmering blue of the river through the kitchen window, the seagulls floating on wind currents. I've often caught her staring at the view with wonder and delight.

"My sister, she means well," she says. "She thinks I can no longer live alone. But I am happy."

Seeing the old lady tear up makes my own eyes water. I forget about the senator handcuffed in the basement for a minute.

"How can I help?" I ask.

She dabs her rheumy eyes with the edge of a cloth napkin. "Tell her I am good with you and Layla."

"I will. I promise."

"That is all I have to say, dear troubled boy. I must rest now."

I take a last swallow of her herbal medicine, pat her bony shoulder affectionately. At least she didn't ask me about the ring. I walk downstairs as quietly as I can, so as not to stir the other Moles.

But I forget about the creaky floorboard by my apartment. I'm about to insert my key in the lock when I hear the door across the lobby open.

"Oh, hey Robb," Aliston says. "Crazy stuff going down."

I desperately want to ignore him, but he's on my alibi list.

"What's up?"

"That senator I work for? She's missing."

"Really?" My pulse starts throbbing again. "Are the cops out looking?"

"I don't think so. The chief of staff went looking for her at a condo in town where she was staying and she wasn't there. He messaged the staff about 30 minutes ago. We're supposed to keep it quiet."

"Anything on the news?" I ask feebly.

"I keep checking, but nothing so far. Hey, it could all be a total overreaction. If I was her, I'd want to take a breather. She's been under immense pressure."

"Yeah, yeah, that gun bill. Thanks for letting me know."

I'm about to duck inside when I see a Mercedes pull up. Chau

Wong gets out, but she doesn't head for the lobby as usual.

She goes down the basement stairs.

Oh my God!

I race outside and turn the corner in time to see her holding a large key ring. If she opens the door, she'll see Austin chained to the wall. There would be no way to explain the situation. Or stop Sean from taking drastic measures.

"Chau! *Wait!*"

She's standing by the door, looking for the right key. I run down the stairs, nearly tripping.

"My sweet, what's the matter?"

"Nothing, nothing at all," I say, catching my breath. "It's just … that's my responsibility, remember?"

"Oh, don't be silly. I just need a gallon of wall paint."

"Please let me get it. I'll bring it to the car. You don't want to get anything on your beautiful clothes, do you? Besides, that basement is always so musty. Stay out here, where the air is fresh."

She's wearing a leopard-print pantsuit and a yellow straw hat with the brim pushed back in front.

"Ooh, you're right. Whatever was I thinking?"

Chau starts walking up the stairs and I exhale, thinking I dodged a bullet. But then a banging noise starts. It's coming from inside the basement.

She stops halfway and turns. "What's that noise? Is it the boiler again?"

I know it's Austin. She must have heard a woman's voice at the door and is trying to signal for help.

"Yeah, you're right, must be the boiler. No biggie. Minor adjustment. I'll bring you the paint."

The owner smiles. I watch her walk back to her car and take a deep breath.

I slip the mask over my head and enter the basement, quickly shutting the door behind me. The senator stares at me with wild eyes.

"She's gone," I say. "If my friend had been here, he'd have shot you."

"Mmmmph!"

Against my better judgment, I peel back the tape, leaving it hanging from her cheek.

"Better be important."

She nods at the shower stall. "I need to use that. I think I peed myself. Guns in my face and all."

"Don't think so."

"You're going to put me on trial reeking of urine?"

"Jesus. Maybe later. I'll be back in an hour with food."

"You're not a criminal."

"Well, that's a relief."

"I mean, you just got caught up in things, right?"

"I know what you're doing, but you can stop. I can't set you free. I'm sorry."

"Sure you can. You're not one of them. You said so yourself."

"Be quiet."

"You're trying to protect your friend, I can see that now. But it's too late. He's not like you. Not anymore."

"You really do talk too much."

I put the gag back in place, grab the paint can from a wall cabinet.

"But it's not too late," I say, turning back. "It can't be."

———

On my way to the apartment I see Layla pacing in the lobby, worry etched on her face.

I never thought keeping up appearances for a single day could be this hard.

"Lay, are you okay?"

She gives me a hug.

"Oh Robb, the senator has gone missing. It's all over TV. Do you know anything about that?"

I can't lie to her. I just can't. I also can't tell her the truth. For Sean's sake.

"Lay, I'll tell you everything I know very soon, I promise. You just have to trust me."

"I'm worried," she says. "*Please, please, please* do the right thing."

"I'm sorry you're worried, but I can't talk right now. I have to think."

I give her a kiss. Maybe for the last time. Then I open the door to No. 1 and throw myself on the couch.

Sean comes into the room and turns on the TV. It's nearly 10, and every local channel has live reports on the search that's starting for Oregon's junior senator.

There's an impromptu press conference with Austin's chief of staff, who is standing outside the condo looking concerned.

"I dropped her off last night and when I returned to take her to the airport in the morning, she wasn't here," Westley Matthews says. "I haven't been able to reach her."

"Any signs of a struggle inside?" a reporter asks.

"Police didn't find any. We've been getting death threats over the gun bill and, well, I'm worried something may have happened. It's not like her to disappear. She knew she was supposed to give remarks in Washington this afternoon."

"Could it have been a panic attack?"

"Absolutely not. Anyone who knows Alex would rule that out. She's too tough."

"There are unsubstantiated reports that she and a friend may have left together. Is it true?"

"Let's try to avoid wild speculation," he says, frowning. "Now if you'll excuse me, I need to talk to the police chief."

Sean looks surprisingly cool, standing there drinking it in.

"How are you so calm?" I ask.

"Why not? We got the head start we wanted, didn't we? Nothing is leading the cops to us. We just need to keep that traitor quiet until midnight, then justice will be served."

The irrational confidence. The inflamed rhetoric. It's like having Viper in my living room.

"I saw that you dealt with the owner earlier, kept her out of the basement," Sean says.

"A little surprise, that's all."

"I would have had to lock her up if she saw the target. Can't take any chances."

"Um, right."

"Thought you said you had the only key."

"Guess I was wrong."

Anger fills Sean's face, twisting it into something unrecognizable. Something ugly.

"If you're wrong again, everything falls apart," he says. "We can't let that happen. You got that?"

"Yeah, got it." My heart sinks. It's not like Sean to bark orders and imply threats.

"And stop talking to that bitch down there. It only gives her hope."

"What do you mean?"

He pantomimes putting a gun to his head.

"There's only one sentence for treason," he says with a gleam in his eye.

CHAPTER
TWENTY-SIX
VIPER

SIDEWINDER IS LAUGHING, making the counter shake.

We're at Daisy's eating breakfast and the TV hanging on the wall is tuned to the Portland station. The bleeding heart journalists are beside themselves. Their precious senator has disappeared. Police are puzzled. A search is underway but there are no leads.

It's everything we could have hoped for.

"A glorious day," I say, raising my coffee mug.

"They did it," my deputy commander says, lowering his booming voice. "They really did it."

A young female reporter in Astoria is saying that the Clatsop County sheriff, Oregon State Police and FBI are about to hold a joint press conference to update the situation and call for the public's help. A toll-free tip line is being set up.

"Authorities have not indicated that foul play is involved," the reporter says, "but we'll be getting more information shortly."

Austin's smiling face fills the screen as one of the anchors at the station drones on about her background, including the Marsten mass shooting and the pending gun bill.

"The bill would usher in the biggest gun reforms in the nation's history," the anchor says, prompting Sidewinder to cuss under his breath.

"Don't worry," I say, tossing a napkin on my empty plate. "No senator, no law."

Daisy, wearing her usual aqua dress and white apron, emerges from the kitchen. With a smile, she refuses the $20 bill in my hand. I can never tell if the twice-divorced brunette is being flirtatious or fearful, like the other sheep.

"Have a good one, Clarence," she says, hustling into the dining room. "Try to stay out of trouble."

"What's the fun in that? Thanks for the pancakes."

Sidewinder and I head outside where we can talk more freely.

"Weasel will pick up the target at midnight, if it's quiet enough," I say. "I'll want the trial to start as soon as possible."

"Copy that. The jury is aware. And after?"

I slip on my sunglasses and straighten my TP ballcap. I know he's asking about the senator and her friend.

"They'll be disposed of."

"If I can eliminate the target, it would be an honor, sarge," Sidewinder says. "Fucking bitch."

I slap the big man on the back.

"You've earned it."

———

I'd been in places like this. Too many to count.

Bombed-out buildings, riddled with bullet holes and filled with piles of debris. No running water or electricity. And yet often there were below-ground shelters where people still lived. Sometimes entire families.

This has the same gutted, desolate feel. An abandoned former industrial warehouse, it had been sealed off and stuck on a future list of Superfund cleanup sites. Nothing had been done other than to empty the remaining drums filled with long-banned toxic chemicals.

Meanwhile, the cancerous plume of groundwater beneath the property had spread for miles, according to test wells, impacting several ranches. If not addressed, scientists warned that the tainted water would reach the Columbia, resulting in massive fish kills and seriously jeopardizing salmon runs.

The property was a real mess. The perfect place to turn into a pop-up version of Guantanamo Bay.

I walk inside and see the former storage room where Sidewinder stashed the senator's friend. There's a padlocked steel door with heavy-gauge hinges.

It opens with a loud protest. The air inside is stale. There's an old thin mattress on the ground. Huddled in the far corner is Mandy Malone.

I'm in forest fatigues, a pistol holstered on my hip. I don't bother concealing my face.

She looks at me and shakes. It's unfortunate, but sometimes collateral damage is unavoidable. She's insurance, nothing more.

Sidewinder told me she woke an hour ago, screaming madly.

"It won't be long," I tell her. *That much, at least, is true.*

"Why me?" she asks meekly.

"It's not about you. It's about Senator Austin and her crimes against the Constitution."

"W-who are you people?"

"Patriots – willing to do whatever is necessary to protect this country. She'll be here shortly, to stand trial."

"P-please. Don't hurt her. *Please.*"

That's better. Just like those illegals and antifa loyalists we've rounded up. They all begged in the end. They respected our power if not our principles.

"Cooperate, and this will all be over very soon," I say.

She nods over and over, a bobbing balloon. It's all good. Part of the begging.

"Now you'll have to excuse me. I have a trial to prepare for."

I walk out and Sidewinder muscles the door closed with a clang. He slaps the lock back on and looks at me closely.

"She's a problem," he says.

"A loose end. But we'll deal with that later. Do you have the video camera?"

"Yes, sir. Permission to speak freely?"

"Of course."

"Why record the trial? Why create evidence that they can use against us?"

I smile, appreciating the question.

"For our legacy, my friend. One day, your great-grandchildren will look back on this moment with pride: The time a group of patriots fought valiantly to preserve our liberty. This isn't evidence to be ashamed of. Quite the contrary. This is proof of our courage to resist the deep state. *Inspiring* proof, that must find its way into the hearts and minds of our brothers across this great country."

I reach into my jacket pocket, pull out a stack of papers.

"Here are the charging papers. I'll be reading this out loud. Let me know if you have any suggestions. I still have time to do a few minor edits."

"Will do."

There's a sudden noise and Sidewinder and I instinctively pull our guns.

The thud of approaching footsteps echoes off the walls making it sound like a half-dozen men. Then Weasel's bald head comes into view.

"Over here," I yell, and he bridges the gap quickly.

"Things just got complicated," he says. "The FBI has visited the building where Hawkeye and Echo are holding the target."

"Crap," Sidewinder mumbles.

"When?" I ask.

"Last night."

"Were they searching?"

Weasel shakes his head. "I don't think so. It was a senior FBI agent that I recognized, and he was alone. He went into the lobby and up the stairs, away from our boys' apartment. He was in the building for less than an hour. I believe he was talking to one of the tenants."

"Sounds unrelated."

"That's what I thought – until I saw that tenant go to Echo the next morning. They talked in the lobby. She seemed upset."

"Jesus," Sidewinder says. "How many people have they told?"

"Let's not jump to conclusions. After all, they've pulled this thing off so far, haven't they?" I glance at my watch. "They just need to hold the target for another eight hours. What do you think, Weasel?"

"I think if the FBI had reason to believe the person they were searching for was in that building they'd have sent in a SWAT team and a dozen agents, sealed off the entire block. But it was only Spencer Williams."

"Who's Spencer Williams?" I ask.

"Special agent out of Chicago who broke some big cases a while back – a black market baby-peddling operation and an international crime ring that dabbled in human trafficking. He had his moments of fame, but then I heard he'd retired and moved to the Oregon coast."

"Any idea what he's up to?"

"No, but if he's been called in to assist in the search, that's a problem. The local police are clowns. We can count on that. But Williams is resourceful. That worries me."

"Let them spin their wheels. After we dispose of the senator, the bill will fail. You said so yourself."

Weasel licks his lips. "Well, we did prevent today's speech. My sources tell me Dems on the Hill are in an absolute panic. They see their big opportunity falling apart."

"Excellent. Stay the course, brothers," I say. "By this time tomorrow, we'll be living legends."

CHAPTER
TWENTY-SEVEN
ROBB

FOUR HOURS to go before they come for her.

Cops are now going door to door in the dark, searching buildings. Roadblocks have been set up on every highway and bridge. Helicopters with searchlights are buzzing back and forth. Coast Guard cutters are scouring the waterfront and inspecting fishing boats and cargo ships.

According to the latest news reports, it's a massive undertaking involving hundreds of officers from throughout the Pacific Northwest, just like Austin had predicted.

More cops than you've ever seen.

I step outside and look up and down the street, seeing nothing out of the ordinary. I'm feeling relieved – until my phone buzzes.

"Robbins, this is Williams. We need to talk," the FBI man says. "The senator is missing."

"Yeah, that's what the news is saying."

"If you know anything, this is your chance to come clean."

"Can't help you. Sorry."

"I think you can," Williams blurts. "Is True Patriots behind this?"

"I have your card. If I hear anything, I'll give you a call."

"This isn't a fucking game. Her life is in danger. If I don't hear from you tonight with some concrete information, I'm bringing you both in for questioning."

I'm trembling as I head inside the apartment. Sean is peeking through the living room blinds, looking annoyed.

"Weasel has been watching us," he says in a hushed voice, the volume of conspirators. "In a car, across the street."

"Checking up on us?"

"Probably, but it gives me an idea. He's the former spook who knows about drugging people, right?"

"Yeah, so?

"Well, suppose he gives us what we need to knock Austin out – just in case police decide to search the basement. We can hide her ass and won't have to worry about her giving us away. And then, at midnight, she'll be a lot easier to move."

Lack of sleep has clouded my brain. Against my better instincts, I nod. "Go ahead, ask him. I'm bringing her food."

"No talking," he says, leaving his gun for me.

He heads out and I follow a couple of minutes later, with Mrs. Wong's ramen soup in a brown paper bag.

In the basement, I remove the gag and unlock one of her cuffs. Then I hand her the soup bowl and a plastic fork.

"You seem nervous," Austin says. "Police are closing in, aren't they?"

"Just eat."

"Why don't you prove to me that you're not one of them – a True Patriot?"

She gulps down a forkful of noodles, then stares.

"What's your name?"

"You know I can't tell you."

"Tell me how Mandy is doing at least."

I stare at the prisoner in disbelief. Does she mean Mandy Malone? Layla's friend? Could it be that she's the one in Viper's crosshairs?

"The gallery owner?" I ask, suddenly stricken.

"Wait. You mean to tell me that you don't even know who you're terrorizing? Is she hurt? Please, I have to know."

"I can't answer that."

"Why?"

"Because I don't know."

"You're a liar! And a coward, too!"

I look away, stung. *I really am a coward, aren't I?* Blood drains from my face.

Noticing, she apologizes.

"Look, I'm sorry. Can I take that shower now? I feel gross."

I study her face for any sign of deceit, but I've never been good at reading women.

"I don't have any clothes here for you to change into."

"That's okay. I just want to rinse off. Five minutes tops."

She smiles and despite the circumstances I see the beauty in her face for the first time. She's in her late thirties, with short brown hair and trusting sea-green eyes. There's a small cleft in her chin, dimples in her cheeks. Reminds me more of a concierge at a fancy hotel than a politician.

"Okay, five minutes. Remember, I have a gun."

I unshackle Austin, escort her over to the shower. She folds her arms across her chest.

"A little privacy?"

"Oh … right. There's a towel by the sink."

Moving a few paces away, I turn my back to her.

There's a brief silence before I hear the shower head come alive with a loud hiss.

"There's no curtain, so don't look," she says.

Steam starts filling the air. Despite the dire circumstances, I can't help but think about Layla, wishing she was the one getting wet.

My daydream ends before it can start. With a tug in the small of my back.

The gun!

I wheel around to see Austin pointing the Glock at me. She's fully dressed. Her hair is dry. The shower was a trick.

"You really aren't much of a criminal, are you?" she says, cradling the gun with both hands. "Take off your mask, I want to see who I've been imprisoned by."

I do as she asks, tossing the mask to the side. It feels good to be rid of it, like kicking a bad habit.

"You're younger than I thought. What's your name?"

"Robb."

"Well, Robb, we're going to trade places. You're going to lock yourself to that pipe and throw me the key. Then I'm walking out of here. Nod if you understand."

I bow my head.

"You weren't really going to let them kill me and Mandy, were you?" she asks.

Before I can answer, there are heavy footsteps above. It's Sean, returning to the apartment.

"Do you live up there?" she asks. *"With him?"*

"Yes."

There's the sound of a door slamming and more footsteps.

"He's coming to check on me," I say in a low voice. "And you."

"Get over to the wall and cuff yourself."

I do as she says. Austin turns off the shower and ducks out of sight as the door opens and Sean enters the basement. I don't bother trying to warn him.

"What the fuck?" he begins when he sees me. "How—?"

"Behind you," Austin says, brandishing the gun. "Make a move and I'll shoot."

Sean stops in his tracks, puts his arms in the air.

"Take off your mask, show me your face," she demands.

"Don't think so," he says, slowly turning toward her.

"Don't move! *I'll shoot!*"

He creeps closer, inch by inch. I'm suddenly worried that she's going to blow him away in front of my eyes.

Austin's finger tightens on the trigger.

"Final warning!"

"Meh. You don't even know how to use it," he says, taunting her.

"You're wrong about that. My brother has a Glock. Stay back or you're dead!"

Sean keeps advancing, ever so slowly. He's within a few feet now. And smiling.

Austin pulls the trigger.

And a fist swings through the air.

CHAPTER
TWENTY-EIGHT
ALEX

IT COULD ONLY happen to me, I'm thinking.

The gun control advocate, betrayed by a firearm.

As I lay there on the concrete floor, nursing my jaw, I realize that the gun had a safety and I didn't notice. A terrible mistake. I've blown my best chance to end this ordeal.

"You stupid cunt," the masked man is saying. He's got the gun now. The anger in his eyes is terrifying. "You'll pay for that."

"Glocks don't have safeties," I mutter. "My brother told me …"

"This one does. Oops."

I look over at the wall, see that Robb has freed himself. His face is flushed with embarrassment.

The other man grabs my right arm, drags me across the dirty floor. Back to the wall. To the pipe. Cold steel ensnares my wrists again, causing pain.

Then he slaps me hard across the face. For a few moments, I see stars. He's winding up to do it again, when Robb steps forward.

"Don't. It was my fault. I let my guard down."

The masked man turns, gives his accomplice a withering look.

"We'll talk later. I'm going up to get the fucking syringe. Gag her."

Seconds later, I'm alone with Robb again.

"Please don't let him inject me with poison," I say. *"Please."*

He tapes my mouth shut. Looks at me with sad eyes.

"It's something to make you sleep," he whispers. "You brought this on yourself. I'm sor—"

There's a sudden clamor outside. Engines. Car doors slamming.

Robb dashes to the door, opens it a crack. I catch a glimpse of blue and red flashing lights.

"I have to go," he tells me. I can see the sudden panic in his face.

It drives away my fears.

The police are here!

CHAPTER
TWENTY-NINE
ROBB

I SLIP BACK into the apartment, see Sean pacing by the window.

Police cars are in the street, lights flashing.

"They're searching the block. We're next," Sean says. His aura of calm is gone. He's finally as nervous as I am. "What if they check the basement?"

"I thought you were going to give her the shot?" I ask.

Sean is clutching the bag with the syringe, but he shakes his head. "Too risky. If we go down there now, they'll want to search it, for sure."

Peering through the plastic blinds, I check the street outside but see no trace of Weasel's car. *Smart bastard.* Suddenly, a blue uniform comes into view.

"Oh crap, here they come!"

Seconds later, there's a loud knock on the door.

"Police! Open up!"

Sean sprints to the kitchen to hide the bag as I slowly open the door. I see Aliston's head pop out across the lobby.

The officer studies my face for a moment.

"Do you live here?"

"Um, yeah. Me and my roommate over there."

The cop shows me a photo of Austin. "Seen this woman in the past 24 hours?"

Sean steps over and we both study the picture and shake our heads.

"Just on TV," I say. "The missing senator?"

"That's right. We're searching the block – the whole town, actually. Mind if I come in and take a look around?"

"Go ahead. Sure hope that lady is okay."

The officer pulls his flashlight, starts going room to room, opening doors, checking closets. Even the spaces under beds.

When he's done, he returns to me. "I'm told you're the building manager, is that correct?"

I nod, trying to hide my nerves.

"Is there an attic or basement?"

"No attic, just a half-basement. For storage, mostly."

"Let's take a look."

"Sure, sure."

I see the fear in Sean's eyes as I guide the officer through the lobby and around the corner. As we descend the steps to the basement door, it's like a trip to the gallows. I gulp, feel the sweat in my palms.

I pull the ring of keys from my pocket, fumbling a bit.

The first key only goes in halfway.

"Sorry. They all look the same."

The cop rolls his eyes.

The next one also doesn't work. "Dang. I really need to mark them somehow."

The man in blue gives me an agitated look, then checks his watch.

I'm out of time. I choose the right key and it slides in.

There are muffled shouts coming from inside the basement, but I'm closest to the door. The cop doesn't seem to hear.

I grasp the knob, begin to slowly turn.

There's a loud crackle and the officer's shoulder radio comes alive. An alert. Something about a suspicious vehicle in the woods. They're calling all units to the area.

Another cop yells down from the sidewalk.

"They found a stolen van – may belong to the kidnappers. Let's roll!"

My cop looks at me and grins.

"Finally, a break. Thanks for your cooperation."

He hustles up the steps, leaving me rattled.

How much more of this can I take?

———

I bring the prisoner some water, but all she wants to do is talk.

She apologizes for pointing the gun at me, says she was only trying to get out. Keeps calling me by my nickname, which is unnerving.

"Robb, please don't hand me over. Those people, they're insane. This so-called trial, it's a big sham. They're going to kill me."

I try to avoid her pleading eyes. Her tear-stained cheeks.

"Don't turn me over to them. *Please*, Robb."

The words saw through me. I've never felt so guilty before. So evil.

I put the water jug down, pick up the hypodermic prepared by Weasel.

A half dose – enough to knock her out for an hour or two. It's for her own good, I tell myself, but I really can't listen to her pleas anymore. They cut too deep.

Austin sees the needle and begins to shake.

"No, no, no …"

"I'm really sorry," I say, squeezing her arm. I plunge it in. "You've been making too much noise."

My heart sinks as her eyes slowly flutter and close. Her slender body sags against the wall.

How can I ever forgive myself?

CHAPTER
THIRTY
ROBB

WE SEE A BROWN sedan pull up in front and Sean exhales.

"That's him," he says. "Our mission is done!"

I look at his face, but for the first time don't recognize him. All the softness is gone.

"Buddy, we can't do this," I plead.

"Christ. This again? There's no backing out now. Besides, she's seen your face."

"We can't let them kill this woman. She's just a politician. If the gun bill passes, it's because people want it. They want to stop the violence."

"She's more than a damn politician," Sean snarls. "She's part of a deep state plot to take away our guns, and then our rights. She must be stopped."

"That's what Viper says. But in your heart, you know it's bullshit. Killing her won't make our country stronger, it'll make it weaker. Can't you see?"

Sean turns away, saying nothing.

"You're my best friend," I say, desperately searching for the right combination to unlock his brain. "You'll always be. I need you to be the best man at my wedding, dude. I need us to grow old and sit on our porches and remember how much fun we used to have. Let's stop this shit together. Let's set her free."

Weasel is getting out of the car, some kind of intentionally nondescript Buick. He's looking up at us, tapping his watch.

"True Patriots is my family now," Sean says, slipping the gun into the side pocket of his leather jacket.

"I don't need you anymore."

———

I watch in misery as Sean and Weasel carry Austin up the stairs and over to the car, its trunk gaping like a hungry predator.

It's five minutes after midnight. A cold rain is falling. The street's deserted. The police are gone.

Between the two men, the senator looks like a drunk who needs to sleep it off. They dump her in, close the trunk, scan the block for any witnesses. To my surprise, Sean gets in the passenger seat.

He's gone now. Unreachable.

The sedan drives off. Slowly. Weasel, who is behind the wheel, is minding the speed limit.

Madness. I knock my head against the window frame, hoping to numb this soul-sucking nightmare. But when I open my eyes there's nothing but an empty street and raindrops snaking down glass.

I pull the card from my back pocket. It's wrinkled and dog-eared.

Shaking my head, I tap the number into my phone. There are two rings, then a husky voice.

"Yes?"

"It's Robb. We need to talk."

"I can meet you in five minutes."

"I'll be at the baseball field by the hospital."

When they come, I'm standing in the dark by home plate, wearing a fleece-lined denim jacket. A half-dozen vehicles pour into the parking lot, marked and unmarked. At least they aren't flashing lights and blaring sirens.

More than a dozen cops and FBI agents emerge, then spread out, securing the perimeter.

One man approaches, slashing through the drizzle.

Williams isn't in a suit. He's wearing a navy Chicago Bears sweatshirt, baggy jeans and running shoes, like he's been out on a late-night jog.

"This better be worth my time," he bristles.

"I can give you the senator."

"I'm listening."

"She's in the trunk of a car that just left Astoria."

"Is she okay?"

"Yeah, just drugged to keep her quiet."

"Tell us where it's headed and we'll pick her up."

I shuffle my feet in the infield dirt, now a muddy red. "I don't know. Sean wouldn't tell me."

"Christ almighty," Williams exclaims. "Are you fucking with us?"

The other agents are leaning forward, looking pissed.

"Relax," I say. "I slipped a tracker in her pocket."

"Explain."

"It's a small GPS device. I use it when I let people take home expensive bikes for a day, just in case. Slip one under the saddle. It's magnetic, so it stays put. Basically, it uses satellites and relays the info to my phone."

"That's smart," Williams says, brightening. "Is it working now?"

I glance at the app on my iPhone, show the agent the map with a moving blue dot.

"Yeah, says they're heading east about 15 miles out. Looks like they're taking backroads to avoid roadblocks."

"Are they going to Viper's compound?"

"No, another place they call the 'secure location.' I have no idea where that is, but Viper plans to put the senator on trial over the gun control bill."

"The self-appointed executioner," the agent says darkly. "Describe the car. Did you get the plate number?"

I shake my head. "Sorry. It's a brown Buick sedan. Probably a rental or stolen."

"Who's inside?"

"Sean and a man who goes by the code name Weasel."

"Andrew Hart, True Patriots' security chief – ex-CIA," Williams says to the agents, who nod. "We've been wanting to nail that bastard for some time. Are they armed?"

"Sean has his Glock. That's all I know."

Williams begins barking orders. "Spread the word, get the SWAT team and copter ready, but nobody stop that car. We want to get the whole hornet's nest."

"Roger that," one of the agents says before bounding away.

So, this is how it feels. The emptiness. The sorrow. I've just turned in my friend. Ratted him out. And sent myself to jail.

"So, what now?" I ask Williams. "Are you going to arrest me, throw me in a cell?"

He allows himself a fierce grin. "I warned you, didn't I? That's where all the True Patriots are headed now. But first, we have to save the senator. You're riding with me."

As we walk over to his black Chevy Blazer, his expression softens, making him look more like a friendly uncle than the championed closer the FBI lured out of retirement.

"I was hoping you'd come around," he tells me. "Your girlfriend said you would. Personally, I wasn't so sure."

We reach the car, and I think he's going to open the door for me. Instead, he slaps on handcuffs.

"In case I'm wrong. Get in."

"Please don't hurt Sean," I say, pleading. "They've got his head all screwed up. He doesn't know what he's doing."

"We'll do our best," the agent says, scooting behind the wheel.

CHAPTER
THIRTY-ONE
VIPER

I STEP INSIDE and look around, giving Sidewinder a thumb's up.

It's a former cold storage walk-in, about six feet by nine, now lined with thick, clear-plastic sheeting. The floor, the walls, even the ceiling. It's where Austin and her friend will take their last pathetic breaths.

We have to be careful. Leave no clues behind. No trace evidence: an errant droplet of blood; a fallen hair – enough for a forensic expert to build a case.

No, we'll exit the secure location as we found it, minus a couple of drums packed with body parts sent to the bottom of the Columbia.

I wish I could watch as the feds arrive, long after we're gone. Completely befuddled. Scratching their heads. Our work would then continue. We'll inspire thousands, perhaps even millions.

"Should do the job nicely," I say to Sidewinder.

The big man had placed a tree-slicing Stihl Magnum chainsaw in one corner, for drum-packing purposes. Sidewinder is nothing but meticulous.

"How's our guest?"

Sidewinder frowns. "Fine, now that we gagged her. She was driving me nuts, crying and begging. It felt good smacking her."

"No more of that, friend. We want her in good condition when the senator arrives. She's our ace in the hole."

We walk over to the courtroom to give it a final inspection. There's a solitary chair for the defendant. A spotlight set up overhead. The video camera on a tripod, ready for action.

I can hear the hum of a portable generator positioned outside the cinderblock walls and ask Sidewinder if it's too loud.

"We tested the camera. Barely audible," he says.

Meticulous.

A few of my men had been pushing to livestream the trial and punishment, but I ruled that out – especially the punishment phase. I didn't want something so historic to come off as a snuff film.

The trial, though, will be posted online in its entirety. I'll see to that personally. Holding a traitor accountable, defending the Constitution. That display of patriotism has to be viewed by the entire country. The entire world.

And then the militias will rise. The boogaloo will begin.

Smiling at the thought, I glance at my watch. Twenty minutes after midnight.

"Has the security detail been assembled?"

"Yessir. Two snipers on the roof. One in the woods by the road, several more at the doors, one in back. There's grenades and RPGs if we need them. Enough firepower to hold off a small army."

"We *are* an army. Where are you putting Hawkeye?"

"Figured you'd want him at the entrance."

"Good. We'll want our best shooter close, just in case. And the boat?"

"Gassed up and waiting at the dock. Sarge?"

"Yeah?"

"Leaving Echo behind makes me nervous. I've never trusted him. Too clever."

"Which is also why we're keeping Hawkeye in our sight. Echo would never risk his friend's life. They should be here any minute. Alert the jury."

Sidewinder pulls the radio from his belt, repeats the order.

"I didn't have a chance to tell you this earlier," I say to the faithful Goliath at my side. "Thanks for everything. Helping execute the plan, taking the risks. Everyone will know the name True Patriots soon. We'll all be heroes."

"Dead heroes?"

I laugh.

"If that's what it takes. We're warriors, you and I. Old age is for cowards."

CHAPTER
THIRTY-TWO
ROBB

THERE'S LITTLE I can do but stare at my phone as the car we're chasing heads east through the pines, roughly parallel to the river.

And then it dawns on me that I may know where the secure location is after all.

"Think I've figured out where they're going," I say, zooming in on a digital map with my fingers.

Williams looks over, waits for me to fill in the blank.

"The old Chem-Lar storage facility. I remember going there one Halloween on a dare. It was deserted but still filled with hundreds of barrels of toxic chemicals. Spooky as hell. We hopped the fence and broke in. Shot some videos in Joker masks. Stupid thing to do, now that I think about it."

"Why would True Patriots pick that place?"

I zoom out, show him the map.

"There's nothing else around there. Chem-Lar owned a few hundred acres, wound up polluting almost all of it. They were storing DDT, chlordane, 2,9-D, paraquat – lots of nasty stuff that the government and farmers sprayed on the ground and in the air.

Herbicides, insecticides, pesticides … Turns out it was all poison."

"Oh great, we're going to need hazmat suits?"

"Nah, they finally moved all that shit out a few years ago. It's just this vacant concrete building now with polluted groundwater below. Viper probably picked it because nobody in their right mind would think of going there."

"And they can see us coming."

"Yeah. Even the old railroad line is abandoned, covered in brush. There's just that main road. The only way in or out unless you can really swim."

I check the tracker app. "They stopped there, all right."

Williams nods. "How far out are we?"

"About six miles."

"Tell me when it's one."

He gets on the radio, directs all units to stop a mile from the old warehouse. "Follow my lead. Don't get too close. We're going to need to do some recon."

My phone morphs as a call comes in. I see a familiar face on the screen.

"It's Layla," I say.

Williams cusses under his breath. "Make it quick."

"Hey, Lay," I say, trying to keep my voice down.

"Robb! Thank God! I've been calling all night. Where are you? What's that noise?"

"I'm in a car with Special Agent Williams. It's been a little wild, sorry I couldn't call."

"What did you tell him?"

I can hear the panic in her voice. It cuts me like a scalpel.

"Everything." I look at Williams, who scowls. "Well, almost

everything. I'm in trouble, Babe. But I'm trying to do the right thing."

"I love you," she says. I can hear her starting to cry. "Come back to me."

"Nothing in the world can stop me. ... Lay? You there?" I turn to Williams. "She hung up."

He gives me a sucks-to-be-you look. "You can still make it up to her."

Through watery eyes I return to the map on my phone. *She told me she loves me but I didn't get a chance to say it back.*

"One mile," I say a few minutes later. Williams immediately pulls the SUV onto a grassy shoulder. The convoy of vehicles behind us follows suit.

"Time to make a plan," the FBI man says, mostly to himself.

———

The first part is simple.

Surround the building from a discreet distance and get a whisper-quiet drone in the air to do surveillance.

"Will they have lookouts?" Williams asks, and eight federal agents turn to face me as if they're on a string.

"Oh yeah. And more. Whatever a Marine squad leader would think of."

"What condition is the senator in?"

"Probably a little woozy, but otherwise unharmed."

"What do you know about this damn trial?"

"Not a thing. Viper just said they're going to put Austin on trial for her crimes against the Constitution. I took him literally."

One of the agents has come up with a blueprint of the plant. It's on the screen of the laptop he's placed on the hood of a charcoal gray SUV.

Williams stabs at the image with a finger. "Here, in the main room. That's where they'll be doing it, I would guess. Unfortunately, we can't risk getting the drone too close. We'll tip our hand."

He steps away, surveys the landscape. When he returns, there's a determined look in his eyes.

"There's high grass and blackberry brambles for cover about 200 yards out. Let's get someone out there to get eyes on the building. I want to know how many True Patriots stand between us and the senator."

"Copy that," the top assistant says before heading off with a knot of agents.

After that it's just me and Williams again. He tosses me a Kevlar vest with FBI printed in yellow on both sides, then puts his own on. He casually checks the clip in his gun.

"You came out of retirement for this?" I ask. "Aren't you scared?"

"Suntans and solitaire aren't my thing."

"Yeah, but you're risking your life. What about your wife? Your grandkids?"

"Wouldn't be the first time I've been shot at," Williams says, his face clouding with the memory. "In Kodiak, Alaska, I got caught in a shootout with a former sheriff and an ex-con on the run."

He shows a scar snaking across his right palm. "I was lucky."

"Ex-cons can be ruthless. Nothing to lose."

"In that case, the convict was the good guy. He saved me."

"The sheriff?"

"Nuttier than a fruitcake."

Williams helps adjust my vest. "I'm not putting you in the line of fire, but if we get McNalley alone, maybe you can reason with him."

I study my feet. "He's down the hole like Alice, but I'll do my best."

"How long have you known him?"

"Since like third grade. Our families moved to the neighborhood at the same time. We bonded over army men and superhero comics, and later music and girls."

"Your best friend?"

"Yeah. There was really no doubt that we'd be roommates after high school."

"Why didn't you two open the bike shop together?"

"That was the plan, but then the garbage company called. He couldn't say no. Since we were kids he wanted to drive something huge, like an 18-wheeler or a tank. He could've enlisted in the Army, I suppose. Glad he didn't."

"But why True Patriots? Last time I checked, they have no tanks. What drew him in?"

"Honestly? I think it was those conspiracy websites. He started out just surfing but the more he read, the more he got into it. Like quicksand for your brain. Meeting Viper was the clincher. He's larger than life, spouting patriotic principles and all that. When True Patriots drove through Portland on MLK Day, causing a near riot, Lay and me – we were horrified. Sean loved it."

"I see."

"We went to a militia meeting. I thought he'd see how bogus it was, but days later he's buying a gun and hanging out at the shooting range."

"And winning a tournament."

"Viper asked him to join after that, and he jumped at the chance. Got a code name: Hawkeye. He loved that, too."

"Why did you join?"

"To protect him." I spit on the grass. "That didn't work out very well."

"So far. We don't know how this story ends yet."

He takes out a cigarette, puts it between his lips but doesn't smoke it. After a minute, my curiosity makes me ask.

"Need a light?"

"Oh, no," he says. "My wife says it's too dangerous."

Before I can say anything, an agent rushes up to Williams. "There's a spotter by the front gate concealed in some trees. We're seeing two men with rifles on the roof, several armed sentries by the building entrance."

"They're bracing for a fight, but we may have no choice," Williams says. "A senator's life is on the line."

"And her friend," I chip in.

"Right, I knew that was no robbery at the gallery. Okay, let's bring up the SWAT team and get the chopper unit ready. Get local police to set up roadblocks in all directions. We'll take out the spotter and snipers at the same time, then storm the goddamn place."

"Try negotiating first?" the other agent asks.

"No time," Williams answers dryly. "If what we know about Viper is true, he'll take the hostages out rather than surrender. He's desperate to be some kind of martyr for the cause."

I nod in agreement and look away. My heart is racing. I've never been this scared.

What will Sean do when the shooting starts?

CHAPTER
THIRTY-THREE
ALEX

'WELCOME, SENATOR.'

I scramble to my feet, rubbing each wobbly leg to restore blood flow. My head is throbbing, my vision blurry.

An enormous man in fatigues is standing next to me, hand on his holster.

"Where am I?"

"It's your courtroom," says a tall man, also dressed like a soldier. "Well, actually, that's in the next room, but I thought you'd want to make yourself more … presentable."

The man drops a clear plastic bag by my feet that appears to contain a change of clothes, a hairbrush, small hand mirror and some makeup. Even a tube of lipstick.

Christ. This is some insane shit.

"You must be the one who calls himself Viper," I say, as the world comes into focus. "The leader of True Patriots. The one who makes death threats."

He bows with theatrical flourish.

"And you are the junior senator of Oregon, Alexandra J. Austin."

"They're coming for me, you know. They were all over Astoria. They'll be here, too, it's just a matter of time."

Viper laughs. I notice the TP patch on his shoulder. The sidearm. The combat knife.

"We are in the middle of nowhere," he says. "And time is what you don't have, senator."

"If you don't let me go right now, you'll all be going to prison for the rest of your lives."

The militia leader seems amused. "You don't understand what it means to be a patriot. The sacrifices that must be made. But you will. Very soon, you will."

"You're just a gang of white nationalist thugs desperately trying to hang on to a racist past. You're all dinosaurs, facing extinction."

He scoffs. "Fifty years from now, we'll be remembered as heroes, Miss Austin. I'm afraid you'll be a footnote in history. Just another disgraced politician."

"You're insane."

Viper's deputy takes a menacing step toward me but the commander stops him.

"Sidewinder, show her the dressing room. The trial is about to start."

The big man pulls me into a concrete-walled room the size of a large closet. The only thing inside is a folding chair. He tosses in the plastic bag.

"Make yourself look good for the camera," Sidewinder says with a creepy leer. "You've got five minutes."

Five minutes. Here we go again.

The door shuts with a heavy thud. A deadbolt slides into place.

I look in the bag, see there's a pair of dark blue slacks and a matching top that appear to be the right size. Looking down, I examine my own clothes, now streaked with dirt and dust.

There's no way I want to make myself up for their sick show, but ...

I look around for cameras and see none. I swap clothes, then take the mirror and break it with a stomp of my shoe. I extract one shard of glass, nearly three inches long. Tearing a rag from my old top, I create a handle. Then I carefully slip the shard in my right sock.

Stuffing the dirty clothes and broken mirror deep in the bag, I turn and face the cell-like door.

There's a sound like radio static behind me, but this time I don't look. This time I don't break into tears.

I'm a survivor, I tell myself.

———

"That's better," Viper says, looking me up and down. "We don't want anyone thinking we tortured you or anything."

"Where's Mandy?" I ask with as much bravado as I can muster. "I need to see her first, make sure she's okay."

Stall, Alex, stall.

Viper and Sidewinder exchange glances.

"You'll have to take my word for it," the leader says. "She's fine."

"*Your word?* You expect me to trust you?"

Viper frowns as Sidewinder forms Hulk-sized fists. I brace myself for a bone-crushing blow.

"Of course not," the leader says finally. "We'll take you to her."

He walks across the old warehouse in long strides as Sidewinder, gripping my left arm, pulls me along. Viper stops at a steel door with a small window that's been papered over.

"Your friend wouldn't stop screaming, so we had to take a few precautions," he says, ripping off the paper. "One look, no talking."

I'm shocked to see Mandy lying in the corner. One of her legs is shackled, chained to a steel hook drilled into the floor.

She's gagged with a white cloth that runs through her mouth. The front of her dress is soaked with blood and her lower lip is swollen. Seeing her like this breaks my heart.

Mandy spots me. Her eyes are wide with panic. I can hear her muffled cries before I'm yanked away.

Glaring at Viper with a boiling rage, I calculate how quickly I could slit his throat with my glass shank. But the man mountain is still squeezing my arm.

"Good, you're angry," Viper says with a tight smile. It seems unnatural on his weathered face, a stream in a desert. "It'll make better video."

"You goddamn maniac, if you harm her …" My impotent threat trails off.

"Senator, it's up to you. If you pull any stunts during the trial, Miss Malone will be punished severely. Remember that."

"You're all monsters!"

"Depends on your point of view, I suppose."

Turning to Sidewinder, he says, "Let's get her seated. We don't want to keep the jury waiting."

CHAPTER
THIRTY-FOUR
VIPER

I WATCH AS the senator is plopped roughly on a wooden chair in the center of the room. She's not bound. There's nowhere for her to run.

An elevated platform with seating for six has been rolled in for the jury. There's also a podium for myself, positioned between a pair of American flags on poles.

Nice touches, even if they won't appear in the video. The camera will be focused exclusively on Austin, defiler of the Constitution.

I feel a buzz of excitement as the spotlight turns on, bathing the defendant in white light.

"Any security issues?" I ask Weasel.

"No, and that concerns me," he says, wiping sweaty fog from his thick glasses. "I would have expected more from Williams."

I clasp my security man's shoulder.

"I think you overestimate the cunning of federal law enforcement. By purging True Patriots of rats like Talisman, we have reduced the FBI to a clumsy, reactive force. They're too slow to stop us."

"Unless Echo has been turned."

"That would be unfortunate, but he knows next to nothing."

"He knows the car I was using. I think I'll have them sweep it for bugs before we sink it in the river."

"That's fine. Do what you need to do, but do it quickly. I want you on the camera. The jurors are waiting."

Weasel gives me an anxious look. I respond with a confident grin.

"Less than an hour from now, True Patriots will be securing its place in the history books alongside George Washington and Thomas Jefferson. Now go."

As the little man hustles off, Sidewinder hands me back the charging papers. He's jotted a few choice expletives in the part detailing the gun bill's provisions.

I give him a nod. "My sentiments exactly."

A few minutes later, Weasel returns to the video setup and immediately starts defogging his glasses again. Feeling a rush of adrenalin, I give Sidewinder the signal.

Six men – three in fatigues, two in business attire, one dressed like a rancher with a cowboy hat – cross the floor and take their seats. They stare down at the defendant with disgust. That is good. This is no time for sympathy. She's an enemy of the people, after all.

"Gentlemen of the jury," I begin. "We are gathered on this historic occasion to hear the charges against Senator Alexandra Austin, as brought forward under the Constitution by the People's Militia of the state of Oregon."

Taking a dramatic pause, I look over at the defendant in the chair. See her squirm.

"You, the jury, will decide whether the evidence presented today constitutes treason … which is punishable in only one way. By death."

The color drains from Austin's face. Also good.

"I will now read the People's case," I say, picking up the papers. "Count one. The—"

"I object!"

Austin is on her feet. Weasel scrambles to keep her in the frame.

Playing the role of bailiff, Sidewinder rises, gripping the pistol at his side. He looks at me in confusion, not sure whether restraining the defendant on camera is something he should do.

"What kind of trial is this?" she declares, sounding more defiant than scared. "In the America I know, I'm entitled to a defense. Or is this nothing more than cold, calculated murder?"

I admire her guts. Or is she just buying time? I'd like nothing more than to have Sidewinder break her nose, but the jurors are looking at me and I can see the first grains of doubt in their eyes.

"Miss Austin," I say, maintaining my composure, "you will be given the opportunity to speak on your behalf after the case against you is presented. Be seated. The court won't allow further outbursts."

As she slowly sits, I resume my reading, laying out numerous violations against the Second Amendment, the sacred right to bear arms. I detail the provisions of the despised gun bill, my words dipped in disgust. The jury is with me again, full of fury and outrage.

It takes nearly a quarter-hour to complete my reading. I feel proud. I had lifted some material off other militia websites, but the bulk of the charging document was my own creation.

"Members of the jury," I say, laying the papers down, "the People have proven that the defendant violated her oath to defend the Constitution, which, we all agree, is divinely inspired. By plotting to take away our guns, she is intent on taking away our liberty. These crimes are not only against our great country and the Founders, but against the will of God Himself. "And now the accused may say her final words."

A man with a gun runs into the room. It's Hawkeye, looking alarmed. He whispers in Weasel's ear, prompting my security man's jaw to drop.

"But first, we will take a brief recess," I announce, stepping away.

The jury files out to a staging room where there's lukewarm coffee and day-old doughnuts. "Watch her," I say to Sidewinder, who nods.

Weasel and Hawkeye are standing a few feet away, shaking their heads.

"This better be important," I tell them. "What the fuck's the matter?"

"We found this inside the trunk," Weasel whispers. He opens his hand, revealing the miniature tracker.

"What is it?"

"Commercial-grade GPS tracker. They know we're here."

"Has the spotter seen anything?"

"Not yet. They may be massing just out of view."

I tug my beard, trying to focus. This is a merely a challenge. A wrinkle. Nothing more.

"Okay, they may know we have the senator. But as long as they think she's alive, they'll be in rescue mission mode: negotiations and the like. That buys us time."

Weasel nods. Hawkeye, so young and inexperienced, has fear in his eyes. I've seen it a hundred times. Usually right before battle.

"Lock and load, men. This place is a fortress. We can hold them off, use the tunnel when we have to. Alert the others, Weasel, but be quick. We've got a trial to finish."

"Will do," he says, scurrying away.

Hawkeye is about to return to his post, but I grab his hand.

"You'll do fine. Chances are we'll be done here long before they get their act together."

The new recruit gives a weak nod.

"But if bullets do fly, it's good that someone who can shoot has my back. You've got my back, right?"

"Yessir."

"Good. Now go earn your merit badge. I'm proud of you."

I watch him leave, his confidence restored. But mine isn't.

If he's a goddamn informer, I'll cut his throat.

CHAPTER
THIRTY-FIVE
ROBB

LAYLA APPROACHES in that sexy way of hers, wearing frayed denim shorts and a lacy crop top.

She kicks off her sandals, mounts me on the couch.

"Do you want me?"

Her smile is seductive. Those gold-flake eyes are glowing. She kisses my lips and then my neck, sending her soft hair tumbling onto my face. It smells sweet, like peonies in a summer breeze.

"Oh Baby, you know it."

"Then why did you lie to me?"

"Wait, what?"

"You lied to me, Robb."

Her face is changing, hardening into something very different. Her eyes are now black as coal, her skin a scaly green.

"I-I didn't mean to."

You lied to me!

A hand reaches out and grabs me. I feel my body shaking. She's trying to kill me.

"No, please ... *please don't!*"

My eyes open and I see Williams gripping my arm.

"I let you be for two minutes, and you have a nightmare?" he says, looking relieved. "And on your feet, too. I thought you just needed space, but when I saw you shaking like that ..."

"Thanks."

"Son, I know how much stress you're under. I get it. Just hang in there a little longer."

I nod, wipe sweat off my forehead. The SWAT team has arrived in their black helmets and body armor. More than a dozen grim men armed with assault rifles.

When I turn back, Williams is still assessing me – seeing if I'm up to the task he's about to lay on me.

"I'm going to need you to call your pal, try to reason with him. If he helps us get inside quietly, we can save lives. At the very least, he can save himself."

"I'll try. What happens if he says no?"

"Then we take out the sentry and snipers, send in the chopper and the SWAT team. I have a go from Washington to do whatever it takes to rescue the senator."

"And if she's already dead?"

"Then we all lose. But, hey, have I told you I'm an optimist?" He checks his watch. "C'mon let's get closer, then you can make the call."

"Why closer?"

"Because either way, we're going in."

———

I'm on the ground, back against a pine tree less than a football field from the old warehouse. I search my phone, find Sean in my VIP list.

Drawing a deep breath, I make the call. Williams is taking a knee a few feet away, shielded by blackberry bushes.

The phone rings several times before Sean picks up. I press a button, putting the call on speaker.

"What?"

"It's me."

"Busy. Bad time."

"Sean, I'm outside with a million cops. They asked me to call and try to arrange a surrender or something."

There's a long pause, but he doesn't hang up.

"Are you there?"

"You ratted us out," Sean says, his voice dipped in acid. "You put that tracker in the car. I can't believe it."

"I'm trying to save you."

"I don't need your help. Tell your new friends we're ready for them."

"Sean, is the senator and her friend okay?"

"Why should I tell you anything? You're a traitor."

"We're best friends!"

"Not anymore."

"Get out of there. Do it now. You've been fed a bunch of lies. Viper and his goons are going to murder innocent people. You can help us stop them."

Sean responds with a shrill laugh that gives me goosebumps.

"There's no saving her now. The verdict's coming in."

Before I can say another word, the call ends. There are tears in my eyes but Williams seems relieved.

"She's still alive," he says into his radio. "We're going in. Wait for my signal."

To me, the FBI man says, "You can stay here where it's safe. Or you can follow me and maybe have one last chance to save your friend."

"Are you asking me to walk into a meat grinder? After what you heard Sean say? About us not being friends anymore. Calling me a traitor?"

"Will he shoot you if you're face to face?" "No, I-I ... don't think so. He's changed so much, but I don't think he'd kill me."

"Hey, it's your call. I won't force you to be in harm's way. But I do need an answer in the next 10 seconds."

"Fuck you and fuck all of this!" I yell, gesturing wildly at the heavily armed men moving up around us.

"You're out?"

"I'm in, you bastard. I couldn't live with myself if I didn't give it one more shot."

"That's what I figured," he says, removing the handcuffs. "Stay behind me and keep your head down."

CHAPTER
THIRTY-SIX
ALEX

STALL, ALEX, STALL.

The police are gathering outside, I just know it. It was written all over the face of that little man with the glasses.

There's no reading Viper's stony mug, however, and that's what scares me. He wouldn't fear the cops. Going out in a hail of gunfire as a demented defender of the Constitution, a martyr for the cause and an inspiration to radical militias across the nation, well, that would be his fervent desire.

My heart is pounding. I scan the so-called jury and see little but pursed lips and anger.

Who are they – these older white men? A rancher or two? A shopkeeper? An ex-cop, maybe. Ex-military, certainly.

Fellow Oregonians all, I presume. We breathe the same air, walk in the same woods, enjoy the same sunrises and sunsets, and yet we are worlds apart. I strive to save lives by curbing gun violence and they are so very willing to aid and abet massacres. Even premeditated murder. My own.

Who are these people sitting in judgment in this mockery of a trial? These accessories to murder are unmasked. They're either delusional disciples or just confident that I won't live long enough to identify them. That thought chills me even more.

Have they even read the Constitution? I have. Have they witnessed carnage in the wake of a deranged shooter? I have.

With a fury of my own, I begin to speak. I lock onto the distinguished, graying man in the pressed suit. He's wearing a wedding ring. Probably a father. Old enough to also be a grandfather. Maybe a retired businessman with a good reputation. And yet, here he is, eager to literally condemn a sitting U.S. senator. Here he is, playing the role of executioner.

I notice the small American flag pin in his lapel, similar to the one I wear in Washington. How did it come to this, two different worlds – but only one tethered to reality?

"One of the great things about this country," I say, "is how we treat those of us who stand accused. The right to a lawyer, a fair trial, a jury of our peers. In America, we don't kidnap people and sentence them to death. We aren't a nation of vigilantes, who use the Constitution as a smokescreen.

"In the America that I love and represent, we debate and protest – sometimes passionately – but we don't assassinate opposition leaders. We're deeply polarized, yes, but we don't kill each other. And yet, here I am, awaiting a verdict from a group of radicalized men who most certainly are not a jury of my peers.

"You were all picked by this man – a man who prefers to be called a snake's name and preaches hate. He was dishonorably discharged for harming civilians, this leader of yours. He's been linked to atrocities at the border, targeting migrant families. He's also terrorized people here, in his home state – *your state*. People who don't share the same religion, the same skin color, the same sexual orientation.

"No, you're not really a jury, and this isn't really a trial, is it? If it was, there would be a judge and rules of evidence and lawyers. No, it's all just a show for the camera – the kind of show Jihadists stage right before they behead their prisoners. They thought that was God's justice, too. Cutting heads off in a dank basement. Look around. Does this seem like a courtroom or something out of Iraq or Afghanistan? Are you citizens of a democracy or terrorists?"

The man in the suit looks away. He's human, after all.

Viper, though, is scowling. I can see a purple vein bulging in his forehead like an angry worm. He'd love nothing more than to shut me down, shoot me with his pistol. But then he'd mar his damn video.

Stall, Alex, stall.

"Guns, guns, guns," I say. "That's why we're here, isn't it? You take the Second Amendment literally, though it was written in the 18th century, long before America became a battleground of hundreds of mass shootings every year. Long before elementary schools, like where I used to teach, were riddled with bullets and filled with dead bodies. You take the Second Amendment literally, especially the part about militias and the right to bear arms. And yet you forget that there is always responsibility. Like cars and seatbelts and second-hand smoke. Or yelling 'fire' in a crowded theater.

"You see, no matter what you've been told or read on the internet, I don't oppose gun ownership. My father hunted on weekends, deer and elk mostly. My older brother moved to New York City and bought a firearm for protection. They support background checks; they support keeping guns out of the hands of felons and the mentally ill. And they don't want military-grade weapons to be readily available on the streets of every city in America.

"True Patriots, on the other hand, wants to arm everyone. Teachers. Bus drivers. Mail carriers. Social workers. They want to pour gasoline on the fire raging in this country. They'll kill to get their way. They'll kill politicians like me. Well, I'm not afraid.

"I'm Alexandra Austin, and I represent this state. As far as I'm concerned, you can all go straight to hell."

I take my seat and watch as Viper bolts to his feet.

"The defendant has said her piece," he snarls. "The jury will now render a verdict."

The six men don't bother going to a room to deliberate. They merely exchange glances for a few moments.

The man in the suit stands. He avoids my gaze.

"Guilty," he declares.

Viper nods solemnly, playing the part to perfection.

"Very well," the militia leader says. "The jury is dismissed."

CHAPTER
THIRTY-SEVEN
ROBB

THE SENTRY IS taken out first, just as they planned. Then the snipers on the roof. Nice and clean.

In the distance, I hear the whoop-whoop of a helicopter loaded with FBI agents in full tactical gear. Ahead of me, the SWAT team is charging.

To Williams' surprise, a black Suburban passes through the old warehouse's front gates almost directly in front of us, heading toward the main road. It's filled with people.

"Stop that vehicle!" he barks into his radio. "Now!"

Bullets rip, tearing through the passenger side of the long vehicle, shredding tires and breaking glass. A man in fatigues steps out with a pistol and is mowed down.

The driver slings an assault rifle over the hood of the SUV, but he, too, is quickly taken out in a blitz of gunfire.

As FBI agents flood the road, other people in the Suburban emerge with their hands raised.

Williams rushes over, motioning for me to follow.

The chopper is overhead now. I see lines being dropped for the heavily armed agents.

There's an older man in a business suit among the group of detainees, and Williams steps right up to him.

"Who are you people? What were you doing in there?"

"We're the jury," the man replies with a caustic smile. "And you're too late."

"We'll see about that," Williams says. "Cuff these SOBs."

He pulls his gun and sprints toward the building. Not bad for a retiree, I'm thinking as I struggle to catch up.

When we get to the main doors, the SWAT team is exchanging gunfire with True Patriots defenders who are holding firm. That changes when one of the cops tosses a grenade that blows one of the metal doors off.

I follow Williams inside, behind a half-dozen other agents. The bangs of gunshots are echoing off the walls.

And then I see him.

Sean is crouching behind a steel drum. He's got both hands on his Glock, carefully taking aim as if he's negotiating the course at Guns & More.

"You don't have to do this!" I yell from behind a pillar, where I'm taking cover with Williams. "Put down your gun, buddy."

"Robb, that you?"

"Yeah, I'm here."

"I'll kill you if you come closer. I'll kill them all."

"These people aren't worth dying for. They're sick, Sean."

"Fuck you!"

Bullets from Sean's gun rip into the concrete inches from my head. FBI agents return fire, pinning him down.

Williams taps my shoulder. "I've got to look for the senator. Keep talking, but don't show yourself. I think you're wrong about him not shooting you. Oh, and don't try to run. My men will shoot to kill – on my orders."

He slips away in a crouch, leaving me unarmed and within range of a crazed gunman who a few months ago was my roommate. A lazy, loveable goofball.

That Sean is gone.

And I can't think of anything more to say.

CHAPTER
THIRTY-EIGHT
ALEX

I'M NOT DYING. Not like this. Not today.

Gunshots are ringing out, creating a deafening echo. Cops are storming the building, almost within sight.

I start to run, only to have Sidewinder grab me by the throat.

"Judgment Day," he thunders.

He drags me across the floor. I try to claw his hand off, but it's like attacking a tree trunk. There's an open door ahead, and Viper is standing there smiling.

"All good things must come to an end, senator," he says. "With some minor editing, this will do nicely."

The memory card from the video camera is in his left hand. He waves it triumphantly as his deputy tosses me like a bag of flour into a room lined with plastic.

"Shoot her, then the friend," Viper commands. "Leave the bodies. No time for proper disposal."

The big man nods.

I'm scrambling, struggling to gain traction on the slick floor. He grabs me with his powerful hands, squeezing until I scream in agony.

Then he flings me hard against the concrete wall, doubling the pain.

The door is still open, but when I look up Viper is gone. The sound of gunfire is getting louder.

Sidewinder draws his pistol. I can see the letters TP scratched onto the barrel. Cold fear swamps my body. I begin trembling uncontrollably.

He grins, revealing uneven, tobacco-stained teeth. Looming over me, he casts a massive, menacing shadow.

But I faced a killer before, didn't I? I try to steady my breathing, control my panic.

Innocent faces fill my brain. Greta. Freddy. And then ... Mandy. *My love.*

"I've been looking forward to this," Sidewinder growls, moving closer. The barrel is now just a few feet from the tip of my nose. "I only wish I could make you suffer. Make you beg like a dog."

I stare at the militia man as my right hand finds my sock. At any moment, a bullet could rocket into my skull. But not today. *I'm not dying today.*

"You first," I say.

"You got moxie, I'll give you that." His fat finger curls around the trigger. "Time to say goodnight."

An explosion followed by screams and yells makes him pause. It's from somewhere else in the building, chaos bouncing off the barren walls, but it sounds like it's right outside the room.

For a split second, Sidewinder turns his head to listen.

It's my chance!

I grab the shard and jump to my feet, burying the makeshift blade deep in his neck.

With bulging eyes, he pushes me away, sending me tumbling again.

Gathering myself, I can see blood gushing from his wound. He slowly falls to his knees – a chainsawed sequoia. And yet somehow manages to pull the trigger.

There's searing pain as the slug rips through my shoulder.

He tries to level the gun for another try, the jagged glass still jutting from his neck.

To my great relief, he topples over instead, his face contorted in disbelief.

I summon what little strength I have left and rise to my feet. My shoulder is on fire and it feels like several ribs are bruised. But I have to find Mandy before it's too late.

Limping past the horror-show chainsaw, I step out of the room and immediately hear someone running my way.

It's a man, moving quickly. I tense, fearing another encounter with Viper.

Instead I see three yellow letters stamped on a vest.

"Special Agent Williams," the man says, huffing. "I've got you."

Williams sees the giant body on the floor and my bloodied top, then nods in admiration.

"Mandy?" I ask through clenched teeth.

"We have her. She's safe."

"Oh, thank God."

"Your nightmare is over," says the FBI man, now serving as my crutch. "Let's get you out of here."

229

CHAPTER
THIRTY-NINE
SEAN

'ROBB, STILL THERE?'

There's silence for a few seconds, then a small voice. It sounds full of fear – so unlike my own.

"Yeah, still here."

"You should leave. You don't have the stomach for it."

An FBI agent to my right is creeping forward, hoping to flank me. I fire a coupla shots and he retreats behind a barricade of steel drums and splintered wood.

The feds took out the generator when they attacked, knocking out the lights. In front of me are only shifting shadows. There's at least eight of them, but none are getting past me to reach the basement and the tunnel. Those are my orders. I won't fail.

For once, I feel certain. Locked in. The gun in my hand feels like justice. No matter how this turns out, it's clear to me now that in time what happens here will be remembered with awe.

Like the Alamo.

Or Little Bighorn.

I slip a fresh clip in the Glock, survey the helmeted heads bobbing like ducks less than 50 feet away. My new real-life target range.

Robb is saying something about surrendering, but he knows nothing about the burden of patriotism. The high price of defending freedom.

"I've found my purpose!" I shout.

Then I close my eyes, visualizing what happens next: sprinting across the concrete expanse and leaping the barrier; killing them all at close range.

It's so perfect, I can't help but smile. My life before was worthless, insignificant. A grain of sand.

But at this precise moment, my existence has meaning. Something bigger than myself. Much, much bigger. A noble cause. And if it takes the ultimate sacrifice to prove that, well, so be it.

An FBI man on a bullhorn is ordering me to lay down my weapon, saying it's my last chance. That's funny. I was about to tell him the same thing.

"HOO-AH!"

With a fierce yell I leap into the gap, firing a sweeping burst.

I'm crossing the floor, watching agents fall, and it's so sweet. The finale on the Fourth. A mad burst of adrenalin and hellfire.

I'm about to jump onto the pile and fulfill my destiny when several bullets tear into my chest. I hit the ground hard, the gun tumbling from my right hand.

My vision begins to dim and I struggle to breathe. A crimson pool spreads from my wounds.

I can see Robb standing, looking at me in horror, as the concrete floor around me shifts, becoming something else.

Suddenly, I'm outside my body, watching myself share a couch with Robb.

We're playing a video game, laughing and giving each other high fives. My hair is shaggy. Pot smoke drifts across the living room.

It's a pleasant scene, this final memory. But then it fades and I realize with a final shudder that I was wrong about Viper all along.

Robb was trying to save me.

My lips move, forming words nobody can hear.

My best friend.

CHAPTER
FORTY
ROBB

THE OLD SEAN, my friend, would have listened to the man with the bullhorn. He'd have figured the jig was up.

But the skinhead crouching behind the drum isn't that person. He'd become something else. He'd lost all capacity for rational thought.

There's only allegiance to a warped and dangerous cause – his new call of duty.

I watch in terror as he jumps out and opens fire. He sprints toward the feds. And smiles.

Hoo-ah!

The first bullets fired by the agents don't stop him. The second volley does.

Within reach of the police line, he crashes to the ground.

I stand and his eyes catch mine. For an instant, it seems, he's the old Sean. And then he's gone.

I'm numb, rocking back and forth as the shock waves hit.

Williams approaches with Austin.

"You did all you could," the agent says. "Remember that."

Words escape me. I failed my friend. I couldn't unlock the spell, break its hold over him.

Austin steps in front of me, looks into my reddened eyes.

"I'm told you made the call."

All I can do is nod.

"You helped save my life," she says. "And Mandy's. Despite everything, I'm grateful."

"C'mon senator," Williams says gently. "Let's get you to a medic."

I follow them out to a frenetic scene of police vehicles, evidence vans and ambulances. Along the main road, satellite TV trucks have taken positions as reporters offer frantic live sound bites. A news helicopter hovers above, catching the bodies being hauled out on gurneys.

Williams helps pack Austin into the back of an ambulance, telling her Mandy is on the way to the hospital, too.

He returns with a radio in his hand and a serious look on his face.

"Viper and Weasel got away," he says.

"Fuck." "We'll get them. They can't get far. Agents are en route to his compound."

"What about Sidewinder?"

"Dead. You can thank a pissed-off senator for that."

That's somehow not surprising. I remember how she grabbed my gun in the basement, had me lock myself to the pipe.

"She's a badass," I say.

CHAPTER
FORTY-ONE
VIPER

I'M NOT RUNNING.

Cowards run. Fools run.

Besides, it's just like Weasel said. An underground path leading straight to a hidden dock, where a powerboat is fueled and ready.

I smile. The country's No. 1 threat to gun rights is dead and soon her traitorous bill will crumble into dust. The video that will bring me legendary status is on the compact memory card in my pocket.

By now, the feds will be swarming over my ranch house, thinking I'd show up there first. Maybe make a final stand. When they get to the barn, they'll find a nasty surprise. Forty pounds of explosives set to detonate 10 seconds after they open the doors. I wish I could see it, the fireball of death, but you can't have everything.

I'm walking through the concrete tunnel at a brisk pace, but not running. Weasel is at my side with a flashlight, constantly looking behind. Looking scared.

I don't even have my gun out. I know nobody is following. The only sounds are the echoes of our own footsteps as we move toward the moonlight and a lightly forested river bank.

"Don't worry, my friend," I say. "By the time they discover the tunnel, we'll be at sea, on the Pandora."

The Pandora is an Indonesian-flagged ship loaded with cargo containers that at this precise moment should be leaving the mouth of the Columbia, bound for Singapore. It'll pause, though, for us.

Weasel had arranged for our passage with a bribe, paid for by a portion of the cash True Patriots has raised from the good people of Oregon. The rest of the money will finance a comfortable life off the grid, supplemented by some occasional mercenary work. It's a skill I prefer not to let rust.

We're at the end of the tunnel, splashing through puddles and mud. Weasel checks his watch and relaxes a bit. "There's the Bayliner," he says. "We should make the rendezvous on time."

I see the sleek white boat tethered to the old pier, screened by a row of red alders. He rushes ahead, starts loosening the lines. I unsnap the strap on my holster.

When we're both aboard, I give him a smile.

"Is the bag with the cash below deck?" I ask.

"As we planned," he says.

"Thank you."

Then I shoot him in the head.

My life on the run just got a little more comfortable. I push his wiry body over the side into the icy shallows. There's a touch of sadness as I see his face slowly sink, but only a touch.

Like most things Weasel handled, the escape plan was air-tight, I knew. Paid for in cash, through only trusted connections. Too bad he couldn't come along, but there really wasn't enough money to go around.

There's the other thing, too. He was always worried about this or that. Probably would have tried to convince me not to post the video, telling me it could be traced using sophisticated software.

Well, he's gone, and soon the world will come to revere the sacrifice of every True Patriot.

My thoughts turn to how much my men loved "The Warrior Song," an ode to military courage and camaraderie. They'd play guitar and sing along. Now it's my turn:

I bask in the glow of the rising war,
Lay waste to the ground of an enemy shore,
Wade through the blood spilled on the floor,
And if another one stands I'll kill some more.

The key is in the ignition. I turn it, hear the Evinrude growl like a hungry lion.

Scanning the horizon, I ease the boat through marshes into the deep blue of the river. There are no rifle-toting FBI agents in Zodiacs. Only open water and the cover of darkness.

I am a soldier and I'm marching on.
I am a warrior and this is my song.

With a deep-throated rumble, the Bayliner heads west to the ocean.

CHAPTER
FORTY-TWO
ROBB

THE EXISTENCE of the tunnel beneath the old warehouse came as a surprise.

It wasn't on the blueprint. The entrance in the basement was behind a sliding wall, designed to conceal the illegal dumping that the passageway had enabled for decades.

Investigators discovered the tunnel when they searched the waterfront, spotted Weasel's sodden corpse and then backtracked. Muddy footprints led to the exit, partially covered in vines.

Williams was already incensed that Viper had wired his command post to explode, triggering a blast that had seriously injured three agents. One was in critical condition.

It was a diversion. A costly one, because the FBI didn't realize Viper had made his escape by boat nearly an hour earlier. An awfully big head start for a man trained in survival skills.

So Williams is in a terrible mood when we're in his SUV heading back to Astoria. He had figured that Viper was bound for the ocean, but it was only a hunch. The Columbia is an extremely long river, reaching as far north as the mountains of British Columbia, where the militia leader could also slip away.

The break comes when the Coast Guard in Astoria calls, patched through to his hands-free phone.

They've spotted a man in a powerboat headed downriver fast and have also noticed that a cargo ship has slowed to a crawl in open ocean a few miles away. They want to know if those facts could be related to the all-points bulletin issued for the capture of Clarence Elias Branch, aka Viper.

"That's him!" Williams says, suddenly elated. "It's got to be. Board that ship and nab him if he comes aboard. If not, stop him any way you can – even if you have to blow him out of the water."

"Our fast-response cutter is already in position."

"Excellent. I'm headed your way. Remember: He's armed and dangerous."

"Copy that."

Williams radios in the update, directing FBI agents to the Coast Guard dock off downtown Astoria, but advising police to maintain their roadblocks, just in case.

To me, he says, "Mind tagging along one more time?"

He didn't bother with handcuffs on this ride. Maybe he trusts me a little now. Or just knows how much I'm hurting.

"To see Viper go down? Hell, yeah."

There's nothing that would give me greater pleasure than to witness the arrest of the man who filled Sean's head with poison and lured him to his death.

When we get there, the dock is empty. It's not quite dawn and there's a trace of frost on the old wood planks. The only people moving around are a few homeless men trying to keep warm.

"I should be putting you in a holding cell," Williams says,

looking pensively over the water. "You're a key witness, an admitted kidnapper and a serious flight risk."

"Why don't you?"

He puts another unlit cigarette between his lips.

"Gut feeling, I guess. I just don't picture you running. Not after the call and everything."

"That's interesting. I pegged you as a by-the-book guy. Why take a chance?"

"We retirees don't like painting by numbers. I had a feeling when I met you at the bike store that you were going to wind up helping us."

"So now what?"

"I'll give you 24 hours," he says, letting the cig dangle like a cool Morgan Freeman. "Get your affairs in order, say your goodbyes. You may be gone for a while."

I don't bother pleading my case for a light sentence. Not here, on a deserted dock. That'll come later.

"Appreciate it."

"Just be ready when I pick you up at your apartment tomorrow at 6 a.m."

One more day of freedom.

His words should have eased my suffering, dulled the razor's edge of my loss. Instead, I feel nothing at all. Just numbness.

"Tell me something," I ask. "Am I a good guy or a bad guy?"

He shrugs. "The story's not told yet. There are more pages to turn."

"I feel like the bad guy."

The FBI man sighs, places a consoling hand on my back.

"Get outta here, Robbins. Forget about Viper. Go see your girl."

SUVs with tinted windows are arriving, filled with federal agents. I start jogging toward the River Vista.

He didn't have to tell me twice.

CHAPTER
FORTY-THREE
VIPER

THE CARGO SHIP with its towering stacks of blue and red containers is waiting for me, right on schedule.

As the sun begins to rise and the first golden rays gild the Pacific, I slip on my camo sunglasses and gun the Bayliner through the miles-wide mouth of the Columbia.

The speed and the waves make the bow of the boat dance.

For the first time, I look back. There's nothing but open water. I should be relieved, but I feel more like Weasel, wondering if it's a trap.

Too damn easy.

The feds must have traced my escape by now, seen the body by the pier. And yet, here I am, moments from boarding a ship bound for Indonesia, where I intend to slip into the jungle and disappear.

Pulling alongside the massive freighter like a pilot boat, I drift and listen. There's only a whistling breeze.

A long rope ladder unfurls against the hull. I grab the money bag and sling it over my shoulder. Then I begin to climb.

It takes a while to make it to the deck some three stories above. As I near the top, I turn to make one last check. There's still nothing but water and coastline.

Maybe the cops pursuing me are even bigger fools than I thought.

I hope the captain has some single malt or well-aged rum on board. I'll be wanting to celebrate.

Hands help pull me onto the deck, and I'm grinning when I look up.

Except the men before me are in crisp white uniforms and I'm in the sights of their assault rifles.

"Coast Guard! You're under arrest!"

I can now see the cutter on the opposite side of the Pandora that had been hidden from my view.

Clever. They planned to take me by surprise.

Take me alive.

I slowly raise my hands.

One of the Coasties grabs my gun. Then come the handcuffs. They're awfully pleased with themselves, judging by the looks on their fresh faces. But they're water cops who spend most of their time rescuing commercial fishermen in distress.

None are combat veterans, I can tell.

My guys wouldn't have missed the *other* gun, the smaller one, strapped to my calf.

As I'm pushed across the deck to the cutter, I can hear the lieutenant proudly radioing in.

"We have him. No sir. No problem at all."

I'll kill him first.

CHAPTER
FORTY-FOUR
ROBB

LAYLA COMES RUNNING out to me like a sailor's wife.

She wraps me in a hug so fierce it knocks the wind out of my lungs.

"You're all over the news," she says, wiping away tears. "They say you saved the senator."

I don't feel like a hero. Not at all. Heroes don't go to prison and they don't fail their friends.

"Sean's dead," I tell her, and the joy and relief drain from her face. She squeezes my hand.

"That's on the news, too. I'm so sorry."

"I couldn't … protect him."

There's a gut-wringing silence before Layla whispers, "But you tried everything. I know you did."

It's near freezing and I realize that she's standing on the sidewalk, shivering in pajamas. We're still holding hands, so I guide her up the stairs into the lobby.

"Williams gave me 24 hours to say my goodbyes," I say outside the door to No. 1. "He'll be here tomorrow morning."

"Where will he take you?"

"Portland, I think. Federal lockup pending trial."

Layla is struck by the news but tries not to show it.

"You need a shower," she says, brushing off my jacket. "You look terrible."

I can't argue. I'm covered in sweat and dust, and tiny pieces of concrete salt my hair.

As I face the door to the apartment, the home I'd shared with Sean for four years, my mood darkens. I'm frozen on the welcome mat trying not to break down.

Seeing that, Layla stops me.

"Shower in my place. It's cleaner," she says. "I'll make breakfast."

We're heading up the stairs when a weird but wonderful thing happens. It's Whac-a-Mole, only much different.

Every resident of River Vista begins opening their doors despite the early hour.

"Way to go, Robb!" Aliston says. "I told the TV reporter that you're the bravest person I've ever met. I meant it, too."

"The love birds!" trumpets Mrs. Wong. "Come see me, I have special wonton for you."

Christie rushes out in her nightgown and plants a kiss on my cheek. "Free beer at the brewery tonight," she says.

By the time we reach the third floor, I'm exhausted. Wiped out. I take a long shower, letting the water pour over my slumping head until it runs cold.

After, the apartment is quiet. I look around, find Lay in bed. She's under the sheets, looking at me with that seductive smile of hers.

"Come here."

The towel is wrapped around my waist. "I'm still wet."

"Do I look like I care?"

After all I've been through, there's no place I'd rather be.

I drop the towel and slip next to her, feeling her exquisite warmth.

————

She's painting when I get up hours later. I kiss her neck, sink my fingers into the inky depths of her hair.

"Coffee's made, Babe," she says, giving me a kiss.

Layla always makes the best coffee – dark, intense and bursting with exotic flavors. Like her personality. I pour myself a cup and take a sip.

"I need to ask a big favor," I say.

She puts her brush down and swivels my direction.

"Sure, anything."

"The bike shop. I need to shut it down. Can you do that for me?"

Her eyebrows shoot up. "That's your life savings. All those bikes."

"The lease is paid through next month, but after that you'll have to clear everything out. Sell what you can, hand the repair jobs over to other shops. Sorry to give you such a headache, but I'll be …"

Gone. Maybe for a very long time.

"How long?" she asks, reading my mind.

I shake my head sadly.

"Dunno. Maybe years."

She steps over, folds her body into mine.

"Lay, there's no sense in you waiting around," I say, pulling away. "Find someone who's not a loser like me."

Smiling, she gives me that *whatever* shrug.

"I'm stuck on you. Like glue. Besides, I've always wanted to do a series of prison-inspired paintings."

"I mean it. Move on. Find some rich dude, buy a gallery and an oceanfront house with lots of bare walls to hang stuff on."

"Tough luck, jailbird."

"You're really something, you know that?"

"What can I say? I'm into bad boys now."

I give up trying to convince her to leave me. It's making me feel even more morose, and I want to squeeze whatever joy I can from these final hours of freedom.

We kiss and I excuse myself. I need to go down to my apartment, pack a few essentials. I've delayed long enough.

I'm about to turn the key in the lock when I see a familiar Mercedes pull up.

Out comes the owner of the building. She's wearing a fur stole, neon green pants and matching sunglasses. Her hair is coiffed into a shiny bob. Defying her age, as always.

"There he is," Chau says, strolling through the lobby. Her high heels clack on the tile oval in the center of the floor.

I expect to shake hands as usual, but she moves in to give me a European double air kiss.

"How are you doing, sweet darling? All that blood and shooting, my goodness. Were you hurt?"

"No, I'm fine."

"But your friend … poor, poor Sean." She shakes her head. "It was on the news. Terrible, terrible."

I say nothing. The grief in my eyes speaks for me.

Aliston opens his door, sees the owner, then ducks back inside. He's probably late on the rent again.

She notices but keeps her focus on me. "Mind if I come in?"

"I didn't want to say anything in the lobby, my sweet," she begins when we're inside, "because I am not a philanthropist or a charity. I have businesses to run. But I am a good judge of character."

I have no idea where she's going with this. I just stand and listen.

"Dear boy, it would be my honor to cover your legal expenses. No hero should have to rely on a public defender. Heavens no. You deserve the best."

The offer blows me away. I figured she'd come to demand that I clear my things out of the apartment.

"That's, uh, amazing," I stutter. "Thank you."

"As for your apartment ..." She surveys the living room and its low-end furnishings with a practiced eye. "I'm going to freshen the décor, maybe give it some new paint, then advertise it as an Airbnb for younger people."

"Good idea," I say. "Definitely keep the TV and PlayStation then. And the games. Throw out the rest if you like."

"Darling boy, the apartment is yours when you get out."

"Thanks, but I can't live here anymore," I say. "Too many reminders of Sean."

"Of course, of course. How silly of me," she says. "Well, my sister will miss you – and so will I."

"Layla will look after Luen. They're pals now."

"Yes, I'm aware. I'm also arranging for a home health aide to come once a week. Maybe that will be enough for now. We shall see. But, sweet darling, who will take out the trash and sweep the lobby now?"

"Try Sinclair. He's always looking for paying gigs."

"Maybe – after his back rent is paid," she says with a wink.

We say our goodbyes and I return to my grim task. I pack a small bag, then pause at Sean's room.

The trophy is there, but my eyes go to something else. There's a picture of the two of us perched on a corner of his dresser. It was taken years ago at a friend's wedding, one of those rare occasions where we were both in suits. We have carnations in our lapels but our hair is still long.

He's got his hand on my shoulder and we're smiling broadly, as if one of us just told a funny joke. I can't remember what it was, but it didn't take much to make us burst out laughing back then. When life seemed so carefree.

This is how I want to remember my friend, I decide. The framed photo slips into my bag.

Then I head for the door and don't look back.

Later, after a nice dinner and a couple of free beers from Christie, I'm walking with Layla by the water. It's cold and breezy, but I can't stand the idea of being stuck inside on my last night of freedom.

We're strolling aimlessly, hearing the sea lions bark at each other among the pilings. A sliver of moon is slicing through a passing cloud. Stars are flickering. It's no rooftop cabana, but it's nice.

I reach into my pocket and pull out a small black box. I show her the ring but don't take a knee, don't say the usual words.

It's far from a jewelry store TV commercial, but she looks truly astonished, covering her open mouth with her fingers.

"Will you hold on to this for me?" I ask. "I know it's not a pro—"

"Yes!"

"You know, just in case you want to—"

"Yes!"

"I mean, think about it. Take all the time you want."

"Robb, you doof," she says, pulling me close. "Shut up and kiss me."

CHAPTER
FORTY-FIVE
ALEX

DOCTORS AND NURSES cheer as I walk down the corridor, my right arm and shoulder in a sling.

It reminds me of my hospital stay after Marsten, only now I'm the senator targeted by extremists as the nation's No. 1 proponent of gun control. The politician who was kidnapped and nearly executed by crazed militia men.

In a bizarre way, they made my point with their brutality and utter disregard for human life.

I leave a room overflowing with flowers and cards, make my way to where Mandy is recuperating from shock. There's an IV in her arm, restoring vital fluids. Her captors didn't bother giving her food or water.

She's weak but her eyes widen when she sees me. Unlike the look of terror she gave me through the cell door, this one is soft and comforting.

"Alex," she says, her voice barely audible.

"Mandy, my love."

Breaking hospital rules, I climb onto the bed, put my arm around her.

"Rest," I say, kissing her cheek. "We can talk later."

"I miss you."

"I miss you so much. I'm sorry. Everything that happened between us, it's my fault. I'll never leave you again."

She smiles but moments later it falters. "Those terrible people?"

"Dead or captured. They won't bother us again. Now rest."

Her eyes close and I hold her tight.

For the first time in a long while, I feel at peace.

———

Wes, who had already visited twice, finds me again an hour later.

He enters Mandy's room with his usual manic urgency.

"Alex, I don't mean to interrupt," he says, trying unsuccessfully to keep his deep voice to a whisper. "And I wouldn't, if it wasn't so important."

I get up slowly, careful not to wake Mandy. I put a finger to my lips to shush him until we can get out of the room to talk.

"What's up?" I ask when we're standing in the hall.

He looks at me, scarcely able to contain his excitement.

"There's been a huge wave of sympathy across the country," he says. "Your ordeal has galvanized support for the bill, Alex. It's unbelievable. That bipartisan support we've been chasing? It's happening. It's real."

"Amazing. I don't know what to say."

"There's more. The president is inviting you to the White House to do a nationally televised prime time address on gun control. 'Tell her to sell her bill,' he said. 'It's of vital importance for the nation.'"

"Now it's vital, huh? Last year, he wouldn't take my calls."

"Last year was a long time ago, politically speaking."

"When am I supposed to turn into The Great Orator?"

"In two days. The Senate majority leader wants to move quickly. The vote on the bill is scheduled for the next afternoon – if you're physically able to participate."

I groan. It's partly the painkillers wearing off and partly the stress of having to rise to the occasion so soon.

"What does our staff expert say? Can we really pass the bill?"

"Henderson thinks the last domino that will fall is your speech. Republicans are starting to break ranks. They're finally going to resist the gun lobby."

"No pressure."

"Hey, you got this," he says. "All of your speeches are from the heart, none more so than this one after all you've been through. Besides, you know all the provisions by memory. You know the scope of the tragedy like no one else, and you're not one to sugar-coat anything."

"So, you're asking me to deliver a high-stakes speech in front of the president of the United States and millions of people on live TV less than 48 hours after I was abducted and nearly murdered?"

Wes smiles, pats my good shoulder.

"Only you can do it, Alex. A hero twice over."

I'm no hero. But if there's a higher purpose in all this carnage I've suffered through, all the sleepless nights, all the scars both physical and psychological, then I damn well can't walk away now.

"Tell the president I accept," I say.

"Great!"

"And Wes, make sure there's room on the plane for Mandy, if she wants to come."

He clears his throat, but says nothing. I see reservations filling his face, strategic calculations commencing. It doesn't faze me.

Not anymore.

CHAPTER
FORTY-SIX
VIPER

WHEN I SEE the FBI man, I'm filled with a quiet rage.

For one thing, he's old. Hardly a worthy adversary. For another, he's Black.

I forget all about offing the boastful Coast Guard officer when I see Williams up close, wearing that wrinkled sweatshirt.

He's eyeing me with deep disdain, like I'm an unleashed pit bull crossing the street in his direction. Fuck him. He wouldn't know a patriot if that patriot jammed a flag pole up his ass.

We're outside by the cutter and I give him a thin smile when he shows his badge.

"The legendary Spencer Williams," I say. "How disappointing in the flesh."

Williams shows no reaction to my taunt.

"Clarence Elias Branch," he says. "Viper to the men he ran out on, stole from – or murdered. Apt nickname."

So smug and self-righteous. I can't wait to shoot this asshole, but I'll have to wait for the right moment.

He unzips the duffel, eyeballs the cash that would have financed my self-imposed exile. Then he orders the junior agent at his side to conduct another search, right on the dock.

"Be thorough. Strip him if you have to. These guys are good at concealing weapons."

Within seconds, my spare gun is detected. The video card tucked in my boot is also found. Such a pity.

The Coasties look at each other, turning red.

Williams thanks them anyway. "Appreciate the assistance, officers. We'll take it from here."

I'm still grinning as a pair of agents arrive on the dock with handcuffs.

"You won't be so happy in maximum security with a life prison term," Williams tells me. He's twirling the video card in his fingers. "Thanks for the evidence. We'll use it against you, but it'll never find its way to the dark reaches of the internet. Sorry to disappoint."

"A minor disappointment," I say. "Word of what we did will spread like wildfire. I'm about to become a true American hero."

"Maybe you and I don't define hero the same way. Senator Austin is the profile in courage. You're just a cartoon villain who failed, betrayed by one of his own."

"Failed? She's dead, soon to be forgotten. With her out of the way …"

Williams bursts into laughter, making me stop.

"What's so funny?"

"You haven't heard? She's alive."

"You lie!"

Williams' eyes are glowing. He's enjoying this.

"She'll be addressing the nation in two days. Watch for yourself – if they allow TVs where you're going."

It's a gut punch. If Austin truly lives, she may yet rally the nation to support her noxious bill.

I glare at the old agent as I'm led to a waiting van.

"You can't stop the movement!" I yell. "True Patriots will rise again!"

Williams shakes his head.

"You'll see all your pals in prison. You'll rot there together."

CHAPTER
FORTY-SEVEN
ROBB

THE INTERVIEW ROOM in the federal lockup in Portland is a disappointment. There isn't one of those two-way mirrors, like in the movies. No good cop-bad cop routine.

Just Williams sipping heavily sugared black coffee across the table. He's got a digital recorder running with a microphone set up between us.

It hasn't been easy, all this remembering. The FBI man is thorough, drilling down and down. He wants to know everything about Sean's sudden dark slide. About the rabbit hole and what sucked him in.

I tell him all I know, but there are always more questions. Hours and hours of questions. In this place, there's no way to tell time and I no longer have a cellphone or watch.

"We're almost done, Robb," Williams says. We're on a first-name basis now, which kinda takes the edge off, I guess. "A couple more hours. Do you want to keep going or pick it up in the morning?"

"Keep going," I say.

He nods, stretches his arms over his head. "Let's take five, then I'll be asking you more about Clarence Branch. How are your high-priced lawyers working out? They seem … capable."

I chuckle. "They're unhappy with me. They want to fight, but I want to get it over with and plead guilty."

"It's your choice."

"Yeah, I told them I want to admit to everything – as soon as possible. At the arraignment."

"I admire that. At sentencing you can argue for leniency."

"Will I see you there?"

"Wouldn't miss it."

"Cool. Hey, I've been meaning to ask: When you came into my shop that day and I refused to help, what made you think I'd change my mind?"

He strokes his mustache but doesn't answer.

"Was it that instinct of yours?" I ask, persisting. "Your talk with Layla?"

Williams sighs, checks to make sure the recorder is off.

"Talisman called me. Told me you'd just paid him a visit. He'd been working for us for a while, but Viper got wind of it, forced him out – nearly killed him."

"That moonshiner dude was an informer?"

"Let's just say he'd pass on valuable information from time to time. He knew you were just trying to help your friend. That's why I figured you'd come around. Sure took you long enough."

"Sorry about that. I was looking out for Sean, or at least I thought I was."

"Fortunately, we were able to retrieve some computer files from the fire at Viper's home, including the True Patriots membership list. We've been rounding them up. The attorney general wants a racketeering indictment. I just want this militia busted up for good."

With a sad shake of his head, he tells me that the so-called jury foreman – the older man in the suit – was the former mayor of Crestview, a developer and far-right conspiracy theorist who once accused liberal Democrats of putting mind-control chemicals in the town's water supply. He was a True Patriots member, the one who owned the old warehouse property. He's now facing a conspiracy charge.

"They're like buzzing flies," Williams says. "But we'll swat as many as we can. Ready to continue?"

"One more question." I was enjoying the role reversal and wanted it to last a few moments longer. "After this, what's next? Another big case?"

"Nah, I think I'll write a crime novel. Put it on a shelf in my wife's bookstore. Maybe do one of those readings."

The image makes me snort. I can't tell if he's being serious or not.

Williams reaches over to turn on the machine.

"Now, tell me about Viper," he says.

CHAPTER
FORTY-EIGHT
ALEX

WHEN YOU WALK into a room at the White House with the president of the United States, it's a special feeling.

And when the cameras are rolling and *he* introduces *you*? It makes you want to start pinching yourself.

I step to the podium in the East Room. The teleprompters are off, and there are more TV cameras than I've ever seen.

It's risky giving a major address with only handwritten notes, jotted on scrap paper during my flight, but I'm not worried about gaffes. Wes is right. Everything I need to say is in my heart.

I look down, see Mandy in the front row and it fills me with confidence. Tuning out the pain in my shoulder and ribs, I begin.

"Good evening, my fellow Americans. Thank you, Mr. President, for your kind words, and thank you to the many people across the country who have offered their prayers and support. I am eternally grateful.

"A short time ago, I was abducted after speaking out against gun violence at a town hall meeting in a small Oregon town. The kidnappers were members of a far-right militia group calling itself

True Patriots. They are anything but patriotic. They are nothing more than violent extremists bent on overthrowing our democracy. In a desperate attempt to stop passage of the Mass Shooting Prevention Act, they held me at gunpoint in a basement for 24 hours before taking me to an abandoned warehouse.

"There, they conducted what they called a 'trial.' The leader of True Patriots served as the prosecutor. Six militia members and sympathizers acted as the jury. They sentenced me to death and ordered my execution. The bullet that tore through my shoulder was meant for my head. I fought back and managed to survive …"

Members of the audience rise as one, erupting in hearty applause. Mandy is on her feet, smiling.

"I am being called a hero, but I'm no hero," I continue after a couple of minutes. "I'm a survivor, one of thousands and thousands. A survivor of the epidemic of gun violence threatening to rip this nation apart. In America, we have more guns and mass shootings than any country in the world by far. I should know: I've survived both a murder plot and a school massacre.

"In tiny Marsten, the gunman bought his assault rifle shortly after his 18th birthday, despite a history of threatening behavior and serious mental health issues. By God's grace I survived the shooting that left 24 children, three teachers and an administrator dead. I was a teacher then, 2 ½ years ago, but I vowed to do all I could to prevent further tragedies. My path led me to a seat in the U.S. Senate and to propose a bill, the Mass Shooting Prevention Act.

"The president just called the bill 'overdue,' but that's an understatement. It was overdue decades ago. It's now become essential, like air and water. There's a uniquely American carnage underway, a cancer destroying the fabric of our society, and it must be stopped.

"I know some of my colleagues will say that the vast majority of gun owners are responsible and lawful. I have no quarrel with that. My father was a hunter. He taught his children well about gun safety. He kept his rifles in a safe. But I am not here to talk about responsible gun ownership. I'm here to talk about the dangerous people who are causing so much bloodshed, tearing so many innocent people and families apart. The ones slaughtering children in our schools, worshippers in our churches, shoppers in our grocery stores and malls. I'm here to tell you we can stop it – stop the carnage.

"My bill bans military-style assault weapons and high-capacity magazines. Weapons intended for battlefields. It may surprise some of you to know that we enacted such a ban once before in this country, nearly 30 years ago. As a direct result, the toll from mass shootings dropped substantially. That's a fact. But politicians in Washington allowed that ban to expire under pressure from gun makers. And so, the shooter in Marsten who claimed so many lives, ruined so many families, was able to walk into a gun store and lawfully purchase an assault rifle and hundreds of rounds of ammunition.

"The Mass Shooting Prevention Act raises the minimum age to buy a firearm to 21 and requires, for the first time, thorough background checks without loopholes to expose felons, fugitives, violators of restraining orders and more. No more buying guns off the internet or at gun shows without getting screened either. The bill also expands 'red flag' laws that allow teachers, counselors and others to alert law enforcement to people who pose a danger to themselves and others. Finally, the bill funds vitally needed mental health services aimed at keeping people from resorting to extreme violence.

"Critics will say the law infringes on the Second Amendment.

They will argue that the law would take away guns from ordinary, law-abiding citizens. None of that is true. We've regulated firearms for a long, long time in this country. Nobody will be coming for anyone's legally purchased guns. Don't believe the talking points of the National Rifle Association and gun manufacturers. They're lying to us, just like Big Tobacco did about the addictiveness of cigarettes. Like Purdue Pharma did about OxyContin. Those lies cost untold numbers of lives. It's time we stop letting ourselves be fooled.

"A large majority of people in this country believe more must be done to curb gun violence. I know first-hand. I've spoken personally to hundreds of concerned citizens, Democrats and Republicans alike. I've wept in their living rooms, held the pictures of their lost sons and daughters.

"A daughter like my former student, 12-year-old Greta Thorne. Her parents said she wanted to become a doctor, and not just any doctor but a brain surgeon. She was the oldest of three children, and she loved reading books and exploring nature, and just being a big sister.

"A son like Teddy Paulson, 11, who played soccer and basketball, and built towers out of Legos and wanted one day to be an architect. Two days before the Marsten shooting, his parents bought their son a new Lego kit – a reproduction of Buckingham Palace intended as a birthday gift. That milestone was never celebrated. The gift was never opened. He was buried instead.

"We have lost these amazing children and so many more, their young dreams shattered in a storm of bullets. But their parents want to do more than mourn. As one, they are demanding an assault weapon ban and stricter background checks. They are demanding action, and we cannot simply ignore their wishes. Not anymore. We can no longer stand by and watch politicians do nothing, fearful of the gun lobby or the radical right. We can no longer allow partisan politics to dictate what we do, or more accurately, fail to do, about gun violence. Not anymore.

"We must protect our children and our families. Too many of those deaths were preventable. Their ghosts are calling us. The survivors are counting on us. We cannot fail. The time for half measures and empty promises is over. Too many have died, and countless more innocents will perish if we don't act now.

"To my Senate colleagues, I say, 'This is your moment. Do you wish to be on the side of the NRA, of violent extremists like True Patriots and other militia groups? Or do you want to be remembered in the annals of history as having the courage to meet the challenge, to rise up against an existential threat?'

"I've been shot by madmen twice. I am scarred, but I'm no hero. I'm just a survivor who wants to stop the carnage. Please join me. Thank you and God bless America."

The audience rises again, roaring in approval. Mandy is wiping away tears.

I turn and see the president on his feet.

As I leave the podium, I realize I never once looked at my notes. I wonder how many times people have spoken out passionately against gun violence only to have their dreams dashed. Is this just another exercise in futility?

I've given it my all, I know.

Now I just want to cast my vote and go home.

With Mandy.

CHAPTER
FORTY-NINE
ROBB

THERE'S A TV in the cafeteria, and a group of tattooed men with bulging biceps who happen to be devoted daytime soap fans have just stormed off.

There would have been no easy way to convince them to switch to the momentous debate going on in the Capitol. Fortunately, all the major networks did it for me.

I missed Alex Austin's speech last night but today's vote could be historic, so I'm eager to check it out. I move to a closer table and watch as a Republican senator named Morris Bagwell addresses the chamber in an Alabama twang.

"Now, I don't know Senator Austin," he says, "but she's too humble to call herself a hero. And humble people are honest people, in my experience. So, when she says her bill will reduce the number of mass shootings in our country, reduce the number of victims, I believe her.

"And when she says there is nothing in the bill that would allow a massive takeaway of guns from lawful owners, well, I can't find anything in there to contradict her. I'm voting for the bill, my colleagues, and I hope you do as well. Mercy, what we've been doing hasn't worked. Maybe it's time to try something else."

I don't follow politics much, but there's one thing I know. Almost like it's a law. Southern Republicans hate anything even remotely calling itself "gun control."

The camera flips to Austin, seated in the back of the chamber. She looks almost as amazed as me.

Next up is a senator from Utah, a deeply conservative Mormon. He looks perplexed.

"In my state," Barry Rondello begins, "mass shootings simply didn't happen. Until last April, at a Provo concert. Ten people died that night at the hands of a disturbed man with an assault rifle – lawfully purchased. Some of us, myself included, wrote it off as an aberration. But then less than two months later, there was another attack, at a shopping mall in Salt Lake City. Just last week, a gunman broke into a junior high school. Six people were killed before police took him down. He, too, was packing an assault rifle."

The senator shakes his head sadly.

"It's not an aberration," he says. "It's the new normal, unless we do something to stop it. For the sake of all the lives lost, it's time to act."

The speeches continue, but the network breaks to the studio where the talking heads are buzzing. The chyron at the bottom of the screen reads: **GUN BILL HAS VOTES NEEDED TO PASS**.

"Rondello has just given Austin the votes she needs. Against all odds, it appears the Mass Shooting Prevention Act is going to pass. The most robust gun control package in history. What is your reaction, Anna?"

"Roger, to tell the truth, I'm shocked. When this bill was introduced it was given zero chance of passage. The senator's ordeal and her stirring address the other night have swayed both moderate and conservative Republicans."

"Yes, and Republicans keep crossing the aisle. At least 10 so far."

"Truly remarkable. What a historic day."

I can only shake my head in admiration. I was rooting for Austin, the bravest woman I'd ever met.

And I soon found out she was rooting for me, too.

———

"All rise."

The bailiff speaks as the bespectacled judge appears through a special door, taking his place behind an imposing bench finished with hand-carved mahogany. It's a huge courtroom decorated with equally oversized oil paintings depicting the Lewis and Clark expedition, territorial courthouses and assorted pioneer judges, all of whom are bearded and hatted.

It's all very unfamiliar and intimidating. I'd never stepped foot in a courtroom before, not even for jury duty. And now the brooding, black-robed man looking down on me is about to impose his punishment.

"Please be seated."

I sneak a peek at Layla in the first row of the gallery, looking paler than usual in a black dress that seems fitting for a funeral, which maybe this is. By her side is Williams, who gives me a nod. He'd filed an affidavit with the court, attesting to my full cooperation and willingness to risk my life at the warehouse.

I didn't see Austin slip into the courtroom, but the first words out of the judge are addressed to her.

"Senator," he says in an ominously deep voice. "I've read your statement, and I must admit that it took me somewhat by surprise. Given the nature of your ordeal, I would not have expected you to be so … charitable."

Austin rises to her feet. She's wearing her usual navy pantsuit with the flag pin on the left lapel.

"Your honor, may I address the court?"

"You may."

"Given the circumstances, this may sound strange, but I know that Mr. Robbins was trying to protect me even as I was held in his building. I believe he was doing all he could to convince his friend to abandon the scheme. When he couldn't, he alerted the FBI. He even entered the warehouse where I was facing execution when bullets were flying that night. Those are not the acts of a hardened criminal, your honor.

"There is no question that Mr. Robbins committed serious crimes, but I am urging the court to show leniency based on his good intentions, if nothing else."

She sits as the judge looks at me and frowns, fueling my unease. At the same time, I can't help but feel gratitude for Austin's plea on my behalf. My lawyers had told me about her supportive statement, but to come to Portland personally?

"Good intentions are not a mitigating factor, I'm afraid. The court cannot read minds," the judge says. "That said, the record clearly shows that the defendant alerted law enforcement, assisted the FBI in tracking down the senator's whereabouts and attempted to convince his armed accomplice to surrender at considerable risk to his own safety. To his credit, he has pleaded guilty rather than demand a costly, time-consuming trial. The defendant also has no prior record and enjoys the support of many people in his community, based on the letters the court has received.

"However …" There's a long pause that makes me want to scream. "Kidnapping is a violent crime and deterrence demands punishment – even if the victim seeks mercy. Before I impose the sentence in this case, is there anything the defendant wishes to say?"

The lawyer to my right gives me a nudge and I stand. I have no prepared remarks. I can hear my heart beating.

"Your honor, I'm guilty of everything. I failed my best friend and I failed Senator Austin. She wouldn't have had to fight for her life if I had stopped this terrible plot. I thought I could. I really did. But in the end, I couldn't. And it's all my fault."

I sit down with a boulder in my throat and hear Layla crying softly behind me.

Then the judge dispenses justice: Sixteen months in a minimum-security prison. He tells me the sentencing range allowed him to be much tougher, but he was sufficiently swayed by Austin, Williams and the others to grant a "downward departure." He thinks he's cutting me a break, and maybe he is.

But it feels more like a guillotine blade falling.

———

Time moves slowly here.

On the outside, there are so many distractions. Here, you just think. All the friggin' time. *Think, think, think.* Part of the punishment, I guess. Or is it more like part of the healing?

At least I have the letters from Layla. One sent faithfully every week. I've read them all many times.

In clearing out my apartment, she found her painting and cried. Good tears, I was relieved to learn. She's going to have it framed and waiting for me.

A couple of Oregon State ag sciences students attending the Astoria campus are renting No. 1 now. When she goes through the lobby, Layla said she sometimes hears them playing video games and laughing. It reminds her of Sean and me – before we all went careening off the rails.

Sean's mother came to claim his things, then made a point of visiting everyone who lives in the building. I'm sure she's searching for answers, trying to square the suicidal militia man with the tender-hearted boy she raised.

When I'm out, I'll go to his grave, then see her – answer as many questions as I can. But there's no way I can explain how he plunged so far and so fast – a freefall to the edge of insanity in less than 60 days. I don't know myself and I loved him.

The big news is that Spoke & Wheel never closed. Lay didn't want to have a part in dismantling my dream, such as it is. She's kept the business open three days a week, says she likes sketching there. Feels my presence.

Mandy and Alex are a couple now, taking things slow. Sort of starting over. The senator moved her main Oregon office to Astoria to be closer whenever she's in the Pacific Northwest. I'm rooting for them and hope to one day go to their wedding.

Layla also says she's been keeping an eye on Mrs. Wong, sharing pots of tea and telling each other stories. She even learned the legend behind the dragon ring – a grand tale if ever there was one.

Young Luen not only poisoned Japanese officers, she also slipped into a prison where Chinese children were being abused and made to live in squalor. Posing as a prisoner, she freed them all in a daring escape, aided by a kid-sized hole cut in a fence and a diversionary strike on the other side of the compound by fellow partisans.

After the war, Luen was given the ring by the grateful father of one of the rescued children. That man, a powerful leader of the Chinese Nationalist government, said the ring brings good luck and fortune to whomever wears it, which for Luen meant starting a new life in America with her baby sister.

For me and Layla, the old woman foretold, it will be both a lucky charm and an aphrodisiac. That seems a little far-fetched but, hey, who knows?

As for the other River Vista people, Christie moved out – she met a guy and needed a place with more closet space. Aliston's still there, though. He puts the rolling bins out on Tuesday mornings, telling everyone who'll listen that he's about to get rich.

Layla finally worked up the courage to have an exhibit at Bellissima and it went really well. Mandy made it a dressy affair, with champagne and fancy finger food and a harpist in a gown. I'm happy for Layla, overcoming her fears and all. One of these days, I may actually overcome mine and give her a real proposal.

Every letter from my girl ends with a hand-drawn heart, each slightly different. One day, I'll turn them into a collage. Make my own art.

I told Layla not to visit me here. In prison. I don't want her to have those sad memories. And I don't think I can stand seeing her in tears again.

In my cell, I have a small photograph. Lay is facing her canvas, brush in hand. Her hair is pulled back, exposing her long neck.

I love that picture.

Below it is the photo of me and Sean. All dressed up and sharing a laugh.

Love that one, too.

EPILOGUE

I'M SURPRISED YOU *wanted to see me, Robb.*

The pad and pen are gone. She's puzzled why a man about to get released would want another dose of this.

I'm a little confused myself. I try to crack a small joke, downshift into my normal, easygoing persona, the one suppressed for so many months.

"Turns out, I actually like being interrogated," I say, smiling.

She blinks, gives me that blank wall again.

Is something wrong?

Not about her evaluation. She gave me a thumb's up for release, even signing off on my good time, which included a modest bonus for working toward my business degree.

I'm getting out in the morning. Layla will be waiting outside. I should be thrilled, but in a strange way I love her too much for that.

"It's about her. I guess I'm … worried."

What are you worried about?

I take a deep breath that makes my chest rise.

"That I'm holding her back," I say, staring at my ugly sandals and starchy white socks. "I feel guilty, like I've stolen part of her life. That she's standing by me out of obligation or duty."

The woman in the chair cocks an eyebrow.

Try not to overthink love. Just go with it.

She's right, I know. Love is ... well, who the hell knows what it is exactly, but I'm smart enough to understand that it should be prized and not tossed aside like day-old Pepsi. It's a mystical force, like the swirling Midnight Stone currents in my favorite artist's paintings.

We've been talking for less than 10 minutes, but the evaluator looks at her watch, the signal that our time is over. Other prisoners are waiting. They're all treading water, trying to survive.

I rise to my feet, a vision in orange.

But not for long.

———

Beyond the fence topped with razor wire, a raven-haired woman leans against a purple car.

She's smiling.

And wearing the ring.

AUTHOR'S NOTE

As envisioned, this novel wasn't so gut-wrenchingly timely. At its heart, it's merely a suspenseful tale about a young man who plunges into the void of violent extremism and his close friend's desperate attempts to save him.

During the writing process, however, it became clear that *Militia Men* would be far more relevant to the news of today than originally intended.

Two major events influenced this book, especially in its latter stages. The first was the Jan. 6, 2021 insurrection at the Capitol and the deep involvement of far-right militia groups, as exposed by investigative journalists, the Justice Department and the Jan. 6 House select committee. The second was a renewed push for long-overdue gun control legislation after a series of mass shootings, including the massacre of children inside a school in Uvalde, Texas.

In *Militia Men*, those themes converge: A U.S. senator on the brink of getting a landmark gun-safety bill passed is kidnapped by members of an Oregon militia group known as True Patriots. That militia is fictitious, but the threat posed by such groups across the country is very real. The thwarted plot to kidnap Michigan Gov. Gretchen Whitmer over COVID-19 safety measures is just one example.

There are many people to thank for helping bring *Militia Men* to life.

Ann Butler provided equal measures of love and support, both of which were crucial during those writer's block days. She also critiqued and then edited the manuscript. This book is dedicated to her.

I am also deeply appreciative of esteemed journalist Bridget Murphy for her keen insight on matters of plotting and character development, among many other things.

Jesse Miller, Jim Floyd, Jacob Miller, Naomi Mahncke and Bonnie Ross offered valuable feedback after reading early drafts, and too many others to name provided the kind of encouragement that keeps emerging novelists such as myself going.

Finally, I want to thank the people of my hometown, Astoria, Oregon, for embracing me as an author.

To learn more about my future endeavors, visit **williamdean books.com**. Honest reviews of my books are always welcome – on Amazon, Goodreads and elsewhere.

Most of all, thanks for reading!

W.D.

ALSO BY WILLIAM DEAN

DANGEROUS FREEDOM

"I'M FREE and I don't know how to act," Bud Baker says after he's rousted from his prison cell and seated on a bus in the middle of the night. He aims to make his way to Alaska, where he has a cabin and childhood memories, but he lingers in a sleepy Oregon town after falling for the beautiful Jo Jo Summers. She tells him the tragic story of an addict whose baby was stolen at birth. When she asks Bud to return the boy to his birth mother, he refuses – until she reveals that the woman is her sister. Bud risks his newfound freedom by reverting to his criminal ways, expecting a manhunt. But he's already being hunted – by demons from his past.

290 pages. Available on Amazon and in bookstores.

———

THE **GHOSTS** WE **KNOW**

SUNNY SLOPE was long touted as northern Oregon's "friendliest neighborhood." But that was before a predator moved in. A young teenage boy took his own life. Another suddenly disappeared without a trace. As fear took hold of the community, the playground at its heart suddenly deserted, Harry Bolden and Fred Von Stiller knew they had to do something. The aging veterans launched an investigation of their own – only to find themselves in the crosshairs of a sinister organization. *The Ghosts We Know* is the harrowing yet heartwarming story of an unlikely friendship forged in the fires of a community under siege.

298 pages. Available on Amazon and in bookstores.

ABOUT THE AUTHOR

WILLIAM DEAN is a former investigative journalist who left newspaper work to pursue a second career as a novelist. He is the author of three engrossing tales of suspense, all set amid the misty forests of the Pacific Northwest: *Militia Men*, *The Ghosts We Know* and *Dangerous Freedom*. He lives in Astoria, Oregon, where he also writes and blogs about craft beer.

FIND HIM ONLINE AT:

WILLIAMDEANBOOKS.COM

CPSIA information can be obtained
at www.ICGtesting.com
Printed in the USA
JSHW020000220423
40698JS00002B/108